**Two Tall 1
One Short**

CW00866407

Two Tall Tales and One Short Novel
Anthology of short fiction:
The Mesmerist's Daughter by Heidi James
Smokin' the Queen by Kay Sexton
In The Clear by Lucy Fry

Two Tall Tales and One Short Novel is published by
Apis Books
5 Millennium Place
Bethnal Green
London E2 9NL

www.apisbooks.com
ISBN 0-9552538-1-0 / 978-0-9552538-1-2

Editors:
Paul Blaney
Rebekah Lattin-Rawstrone

Typeset by Raffaele Teo.

Printed and bound by Lightning Source UK Ltd.

Contents

The Mesmerist's
Daughter

by Heidi James

To my lovely
girl!
So happy to see
you!!
B.y kiss, Talented
girl x
Heidi xff

To Will Self, with infinite thanks.

When I was a little girl the shabby pink bush of lavender was my hiding place; it squatted in the corner of our garden where the privet hedge jutted out into the street, forming a triangle. I hid there in that arid space, the bullying smell of lavender smothering my energy while I watched people go by, identified only by their shoes, and listened to unkempt voices saunter through the leaves. There were always bright crisp packets and sometimes a sticky beer can full of ants to poke through, back to the street, which seemed to have misplaced them. No one knew I was there except the ants and woodlice; not even the sun could find me. I was safe from my mother, the Wolf. I knew she was a wolf because every night she would jimmy my door open with her muzzle and swagger into my room, her blunt claws clicking like tarts' heels on the bedroom floor, her panting rigid and dependable. The reek of her pelt was heavy like coal gas. I knew this would happen every night, and every day I searched for signs of her grey wolfishness under her fake lady suit, tell-tale stray fur that had escaped the plastic-and-rubber-bonded weave and her vanity. I played at being a hairdresser and brushed her human hair just to look more thoroughly for wolf tricks. I looked for gaps in her pretend skin where wiry fur might poke through. She was very thorough. I never found a thing.

If I woke before her alarm went off I sneaked to her room to catch her snapping and crunching her bones, flattening her snout, cramming it into a flat-face human mask. I was always too late; when I got there she was drawing her lipstick beyond the boundaries of her lady lips, smoothing her skirt over her bottom. But every night the same thing: in she'd come, tap, tap, tap, snuffling under the cover, her stinking breath hot on my skin, and she'd eat all my belly flesh from rib to hip, tearing and ripping, chewing with her mouth open; my mottled gristle gone, eaten dry, nothing left of me just leg, leg, arms and a head. All the while I watched her mesmerised. I didn't feel a thing except sleepy, so sleepy, and by morning I was whole again, like myself only newer and weaker. That was my first secret.

The secrets lived at the back of my mouth and if I wasn't careful could leap out and fly in the face of people close by and scare them or worse — much, much worse — make them so angry they filled the air around me with thuds and 'donchewcommitwivmeyoulilbleeder' noises, and my cowardly ears would lie flat against my thickening skull, making no move to defend me from the fracas, and the secrets uncurled and choked me. So it was best not to talk. My head rattled and creaked with the fidgeting of the secrets, which would never sit still or shut up. By the time I was seven no one mentioned my silence any more, there were no more visits to the doctor, just dance class to stimulate my atrophied brain, although some people, including my dad, tried to coax my voice with soft commands and promises of treats. Like the old cure for tapeworms, he would starve me of sweeties then dangle a sugar-bright chew all red and gleaming in front of my open mouth in the hope of tempting my parasitic voice from its shadows. But like the vain women who swallowed tapeworms to maintain their figures, I didn't regurgitate my friend. The family was baffled because I had spoken till I was four, questions and dull nothings, even when the telly was on, till they said bloody hell you never stop do you, you bloody chatterbox. I suppose she fed me too many secrets with don't-tell seasonings and dirty looks, so I closed my mouth and let her secrets take root in the red pleats of my throat. I was quiet then, silent; mostly I was left alone by the family and they didn't bother me with questions and have you been a good girl then,

Nic? And in my throat, all those unspoken words jostled together, friction causing the stink of slow heat. I went to school, a normal school, could read and write, though no one noticed.

Still I find myself under the drape of my nightmares at the moment of waking, the man beside me a dark figure explained by fingertips, the room — our room — reconstituting itself from my memory. A pack of ghosts linger from my sleep. He isn't supposed to stay here, but the night nurses turn a blind eye, better him here than me alone and screaming.

I was a girl, sometimes I was four and a half, mostly I was seven, depending on the bus driver and the smile he smeared on my mum's legs and how much money she had in her purse that day and whether I had too many sweets or any trouble had taken place. Other ages have slipped through the untended nets of my memory, leaving me impoverished and below quota. My name was Nicola and sometimes it was Poppet or Nicky, but mostly it was Nicola, I was so many things and all of them were invisible.

On the bus that day mum had to pay for me and she was fuming about the price of my ticket to the lady in the seat behind; I don't know if we knew this woman but part of the Wolf's skill is to entrance anyone, even strangers. You don't have to have any knowledge of them or their life, just to be able to watch their every twitch and spasm, every flicker of thought or feeling, then you know when they are with you and when you have to change your tack. You can make anyone believe anything you want when you can mesmerise, especially if you have a child assistant nodding and smiling, pretty face forwards, ape-like and innocent. I had the window seat, my sweaty legs gummed to the plastic seat where my dress had hitched up, stars in the flesh on the back of my hands and my dancing bag huge on my lap.

I knew exactly where we were going, all the streets we passed and the rows of pubs, sweet shops, paper shop and Paki shop. I knew which pub had a children's room and the pubs that were best avoided. I knew all the people; I can't remember not knowing them or when I first saw them; they were as familiar as my own toes. I knew the houses with their cruel, pebbledashed façades and the cracked car in the front garden, the windows with their acid-white nets and the milk bottles ready for fights or the milkman, whichever came first. I saw the same people from my lavender bush, heard the burble as they walked past, the vibrations of their feet in the hedge.

Mother spoke louder so more people could hear her lies: 'Nicola is the youngest child ever to have taken this exam, ever, and you know, she is suffering from a brain tumour, the doctor gives her a year.' She smiled at me and the lady smiled at me, the way people do when they have no idea what to say. I knew to swallow the secrets quickly as part of the act. I wasn't taking any exam and I was sure I wasn't dying, but I knew I must never reveal the sleight of hand or the mesmerist's game would be up. You learn this quickly when apprenticed to someone like Mother. She was the best in the business, no trace of a growl or a howl in her lady voice, no slip or mistake.

'What a clever girl!' The lady was impressed by my huge achievement. Her voice undulated; it swelled and subsided, had circles. The secret stung as it burrowed into my throat, so I went back to staring out of the window as it stared back, blank like a retard. And while the secret roused a coughing fit as it roosted, I wondered if the lady would realise she'd been lied to and remember me, or if any of the people I saw knew that I was watching them. I didn't know why Mother told lies – probably because I was not a good girl. What was there to be proud of? I had my father's dry hair and his predilection to run to fat. But if I was silent for long enough, maybe I would fade away like my voice, or perhaps I'd grow big enough to fit my mother's hole for me.

I met him feeding the ducks and coots in the park. The lake molten in the unseasonable weather, casting a steel return of light into the blue sky. I stood next to him as he dipped his hand into the plastic bag and threw scraps of old bread into the water. I don't remember at what point he spoke, but when I got back to the ward he was there waiting. Memory stills death's pluck, I suppose, with its accomplished illusion of a full life. I prefer the memories of others, and have been collecting their stories to paste into a scrapbook, and make my own. The past is a life you can remake, yet I am not a liar.

My dance class loomed. The kind lady and the bus had gone, and as we walked up and across the street the building got bigger and heavier till the earth sagged under its weight. I let myself be sucked in by its gravity, and landed red-faced and weak-kneed in the crowded, clammy changing room. My mother tugged my hair straight in its elastic and pulled me into my red leotard while all the other mothers did the same and their daughters pulled identical placid faces, eyes glazed and minds at home with our Barbie dolls and bikes, the TV and grazed knees. Suddenly the older girls surged in, swelling and displacing us. We went into class and they changed for the street, cramming their rounded bodies into jeans and shiny T-shirts, clad in pretty mouths and black eyes. They sounded like our fridge vibrating on the floor.

Then I was in class, my belly in a nervous clench, surrounded by other ponytails and bright red leotards, and just one little girl wearing her knickers and vest because her mother had forgotten her leotard. Her mother was waiting in the changing room, chatting about *Coronation Street* and her husband's demand for a packed lunch with two sandwiches, still wearing her clothes and shoes like all the other mothers. Some of the girls in my class had tense little breasts that required the clasp of a bra and so were allowed to wear proper ballet tights with seams down the back; the rest of us had to wear socks, even during winter. We were all still wearing soft shoes though, no one was that grown up.

Huge windows swallowed three of the walls and light spilt onto the wooden floor and over our feet, which we struggled to point away from one another as though each foot was repelled by the other's stink. The fourth wall was covered by a plastic mirror that threw your reflection back at you just a moment too late for you to catch, and when you could see yourself you were blurred at the edges. It was like looking at yourself in a puddle while it's still raining. The mistress told us to take our positions for barre work but we didn't have a barre, just a row of chair backs because it wasn't a real ballet studio but a room where old people went to drink sherry and dance in the ellipse of each other's arms, round and round to the taped music of shiny bands. The only barre in that room was in the corner, where it crouched blindly on a Monday while Miss Dawn's Dance Academy took hold of the counterfeit barre in our right hands, stood heads up, arses tucked in. Then she started speaking in a knock-kneed French, and all I knew was that the other girls understood what she said and I needed to pee, my bladder swelling against my leotard in an urgent nag. I couldn't ask to go while my secrets remained lodged in my throat, so I carried on, watching the girl in front of me for clues as to what happened next to my legs and feet. I did things that I don't know the name of, with good toes and my bottom in and my head up, and there wasn't a safe moment once to leave the room. And even if I could have sneaked off, my leotard and my vest and knickers would have taken so long to put back on by myself that I wouldn't have been able to get back in. I continued to make shapes in the thickening oxygen. My arm up, my arm down, bend down to the ground and up, on tip-toe and not, while the puddle grew in a steady stream down my leg onto the floor. I kept moving as, one by one, the rest of the class stopped, eyes bulging, as they saw my piss. Then the teacher strode to the door and called my mother. We left by the longest route possible, past all the other mothers and all the other girls and the teacher's voice saying, 'Perhaps she's too young for this class.' And my mother growling back, 'Probably.'

I knew I would have to go back to skipping in a circle and pretending to be a goblin or a dog on a Saturday morning like all the other little girls my age, and to make up for it Mother would find more stories and new secrets would roost in my neck, and in the mind of the mesmerist I would have to be the happiest, youngest twirler and exam-taker in the land. I was a very clever girl, you see, and there was no letting her down. Wolfy put my coat on me and, as we walked to the bus stop, told me not to tell anyone about weeing. I nodded and of course she knew I wouldn't tell. Silence was my only means of making amends.

The urine had made my skin raw at the tops of my legs, so the walk to the bus stop made me sore. I stank too, especially to the Wolf with her heightened sense of smell; she had to turn her face away when she sat next to me on the bus. I wonder how the world smelt to my mum, how revolting the dusty fag smell of the bus mixed with my wee and the fat man opposite's pickle breath must have been to lupine senses. At the zoo I read that all canines can smell a drop of blood in a barrel of water, or some similar ratio; that they see in black-and-white, and see fast-moving things clearly instead of in a blur. How did my mother recognise me and my slow growth then? How could she have kissed my father when his beard reeked of fish and cabbage water?

She put me in the bath. I sank my shoulders into the warm water before the cold vacuum between the ceiling and the water surface could suck up the heat. I listened to the rude noises from the taps. I became a beautiful mermaid swimming in the sea with octopus pals who danced jigs with flat fish till I was captured by a sweaty red man who put me in the circus where my most famous trick was to ride on the back of an elephant while blowing bubbles. The bubbles rose into the air and when they hit the tent roof punched right through it so the audience could see the magnified night sky through the bubble holes and everyone cheered and clapped. And I smiled wistfully and patiently, like the Virgin does in storybooks, full of gorgeous forgiveness and tears for the humans who loved me and reached out to touch my scaly tail and rough skin, only to be pushed back by the hairy monkey tamer who was my husband. The audience cried out for me to sing the famous mermaid song but of course I couldn't because the whole time I was holding my breath as I could only breathe in water.

That was my favourite bath game and my mermaid tail splashed water all over the carpet and towels, and soaked the wallpaper. My long hair clung wet like a leech to my back and I knew I'd get it. Every week it was the same game, the same trouble; Wolfy said I never learnt. But I did learn and have learnt. I pulled the plug from the hole in the bath and stood up, wrapping myself in a moulting towel with wet corners as the water gargled away, stealing flakes of me. I saw my lavender bush fuzzy through the muddled glass of the bathroom window, calmly waiting for me to squeeze in and give fullness to its wiry branches, make it plump and juicy again. Close to the ground, the branches were bare and spindly, practically dead-looking, impolitely giving away the bush's age. Without people, without mum pegging out the washing, without dad digging, or Nan and granddad sitting in our fold-up chairs, watching the birds ruck on the feeding table, the garden shook itself loose like a wife whose bullying husband has gone to sea and may never come back. It unfurled itself in all its shadows, and from under its gathers and pleats the creatures snuck out to do their business. Tame leopards, whose teeth had been yanked out during the libertarian age of zoo owners, waited in the alley to steal dog food and rummage in the bin. It still wasn't dark yet. From over the road in the park I could hear other kids out playing, squealing and shouting; I could hear the blind thud of their ball as it bounced on the paving. Perhaps they never had to go to sleep, but that was because their mothers didn't care about them. My mum told me that over and over: how lucky I was to be loved and cared for.

I went into my bedroom and pulled my nightie from under my pillow, put it on over my head with the buttons still done up, and went downstairs into the light of the front room where she was sitting in her chair, her shoes off and her cup of tea resting on the arm, watching telly and talking on the phone. My cheese-on-toast sat on the coffee table, rubbery, thick as a tongue. On the wall above the telly was a picture of the Pope, next to that the mirror that my mum checked her hair in. We had three strata of purple wallpaper, flowery on the bottom half of the wall, then squiggles on the top half, and a stripe of leaves separating them. It was new; dad had put it up the month before to cover the half-moon shape mum's flying coffee cup made in the plaster. All my aunts and the next-door neighbour came for a cup of tea and a look at the new wallpaper. Our house changed all the time, the people and the things in it. I ate my dinner slowly so I could watch the grown-ups on the telly fuck and then slam doors or shoot guns. Alone, I went back upstairs to brush my teeth and go to bed, my hair still sodden, to wait for her.

I long to be loved and cared for. My psychiatrist believes this contributes to my promiscuous behaviour during a manic phase. I am not sure, but he is the expert and smiles kindly and listens patiently when I try to find the words she sunk into my flesh, in a mess of linguistic splinters. I am silly with myself. But the she that I am can only be told in words.

I woke up. It was morning and the breakfast voices on the telly wormed through to my room. The wet sun was butting against my curtains and my belly was fat with piss. From the toilet, with the door open, I could see her standing at the front door, talking to someone in green trousers. She said good-bye and I heard the echo of a blown kiss. Then she went through to the kitchen, her Scholls slapping the lino. Dad was coming home from work that day. He drove huge lorries all over the country and overseas. He had a bed in the back of his cab so he never had to leave the clammy capsule except when he came home. Sometimes he didn't come home for ages, not even for my birthday, but usually he came home most weekends. We had to clean the house ready for him, empty the bins and peg out the sheets. I polished the sideboard and all the ornaments. Mum hoovered every room and we listened to the Ramones at full blast. She wore her faded jeans and a vest with no bra, and her skinny tits wriggled about as she pushed the Hoover. My father loved that look; he would kiss her and caress her breasts while she did the washing-up and wrung out the rinsed laundry. She used to push him off her, grimacing, her skin turning yellow with disgust, so that I wondered why she dressed like that. When we'd finished, the fragrances of polish, scourers, air freshener and bleach clashed and stung my eyes; this always seemed to please my mother. I waited for dad on the front step.

Everywhere was quiet. Everyone had gone to the high street to get their shopping; even Dirty Gerty's busy house was quiet. All the houses sat blank, like masks — crammed with features but with no expression until someone puts them on. Next-door's dog stuck its nose under our fence, sniffing for a sweet like its owner — Mrs Budgen, with her skinny legs and big feet and veins that snagged on her tights — sniffed for gossip. She always gave me a packet of raisins and nuts, with a terrible story of what chocolate would do to my heart. She thought I was a retard because I was mute, and that health foods would cure me. I heard her telling the milkman that it was a crying shame they didn't send me to special school. He just laughed at her and pinched her bum. The milkman pinched everyone's bum except mine; he pinched my cheek. Mother said that was his way of being friendly but I thought he just liked fat bits of skin to squeeze, like little kids like play dough. Most men seemed to.

Still no rain and dad hadn't arrived. Lunch was made and thrown away. She wouldn't let me eat without him. The street started to fill up with cars as people brought their shopping home and settled down to watch *Grandstand*. The kids who lived opposite played in their garden with squirt guns. They went to the same church as me and my grandmother. The boys had bright red hair like their mother and the girl had black hair like her father and me. Her name was Moira. She once passed me a note in Bible class asking which football team I supported. I wrote back that I liked stick insects better because I didn't have any brothers. As she read this her nose widened with her mouth into a smile and I became her best friend at church, but not at school or Brownies. I didn't mind this partial rejection because we didn't go to school or Brownies together anyway. Moira's dad was an artist and painted nudes of her mother. Their bathroom was painted red and her parents let Moira wear odd socks. She had three brothers and her mother was pregnant with another. My grandmother said they were good Catholics even if they were Irish bohemians. They never asked me questions or tried to make me speak. Her dad said I was a free spirit and a child of nature. My mum said they were weird. Once, her parents took us all to the park and played hide-and-seek and rounders. They even played with us instead of talking about the neighbours and smoking fags. Her parents drank red wine and seemed to find their children enchanting. We ate orange ice-lollies and lay in the sun. Moira plaited my hair and her mum helped me put my coat on when it got cold, her solid belly scraping against me. I knew there was a baby growing there, big and round, and not something septic, but still it made me feel sick to feel it.

I was not to play with them that day as I had to wait for dad. I pretended I hadn't seen Moira waving, her black hair or her red shorts. My mum stuck her head out of her bedroom window — she'd been straightening her human skin no doubt — and asked if there was any sign yet. I shook my head and she went back inside with a slam; you had to slam all our windows because they didn't fit the frames, she was waiting for that to be done too. Our house was going to the dogs. A blue car slid past and didn't stop. I thought maybe my dad was dead, perhaps he'd been killed by a bomb or the IRA like on the news, then I would never see him again and I'd be an orphan. That would be no good, then the house would never get fixed and mum would always be pissed off. Then I wished I could get really truly sick and have all my hair fall out and be terribly skinny and have nosebleeds for days and days. Then my dad would never go away just in case I died. He would stay and the Wolf would never come back in my room. I'd be allowed to sleep in my mum and dad's bed all the time so they could keep checking on me. I was only allowed to sleep in my parents' bed when dad was home. That was because dad didn't know she was a wolf and she had to sleep in her lady flesh and nightie. Mum invited me to sleep with them so she'd have two witnesses, but when he was away I couldn't go in there. On her own, she could strip it all off and let herself just be. I tried once to go in and see her but she said, 'For God's sake, child, can I never have any peace and quiet?'

Peace and quiet seemed very important to adults.

There is an odd peace here in the ward. We each have our own room with a door that locks and a peephole so they can check we aren't submerged in our own trouble. It is never quiet here; some patients scream and shout, some just have their televisions on too loud; there are visitors, medical staff, cleaners, kitchen porters, drug deliveries. I meet the other patients in the drug queue. Other than that, I only leave my room for my pre-arranged visits to the park. There are two types of mad people: loud ones and quiet ones. I am one of the quiet ones. Loud or quiet, our little hells are all banal. But there is a peace.

Next-door's dog had stuck its nose under the fence again and started barking. It was black and brown with short, greasy fur, yellow eyes and a greedy mouth. It always wanted me to give it a treat or a stroke so I went over to the fence, checked to see Mrs Budgen wasn't watching, and stamped on its muzzle as hard as I could. It snatched itself away, yelping, and then everything was still again. Perfect, ready for my dad.

He arrived, late, opening the squealing gate with his heavy bag over his shoulder, his jacket open and his face red and sweaty with the sun. Then he saw me and smiled, and I ran to him and held his legs and he ruffled my hair. He smelt of fish and old perfume. Mum opened the front door behind me. I heard her standing there, just watching, not saying hello or how are you. I followed dad up the garden path and watched how she kept her eyes open when he kissed her, even when he put his tongue in her mouth. She was watching for danger maybe, or rain.

Inside the house, in the front room, he rummaged through his bag for presents while she put the kettle on. 'There you go, treasure.' He pulled out a toy camera, which was really a key ring – when you held it up to the light and pressed the button, pictures of naked women with flowers in their hair appeared in the tiny eye-hole. For my mother there was a bottle of perfume with white doves on the box. He pulled us both onto his lap for a cuddle, and I rested against his smell and the sound of his breathing, holding tight to my new camera.

'I'll get the tea.' Mum went to the kitchen. I stayed in the warmth of his lap, felt him alive and separate under me. The house settled, found quiet, and stopped its rattle. The living room's angles smudged; everywhere was soft. My body smoothed itself out, unravelled. We were alone and he was mine. Then he shrugged me off, all floppy, and followed her out.

Then sounds began again. The house trembled with noise, the garden roared and voices, constant voices, chatter and chatter, natter natter. I heard my voice there in my head amidst it all; I recognised it, my own strange bray, could taste and measure its weight with my tongue. All the unsaid words strung together like glass beads. The kettle boiled somewhere outside of me.

In the kitchen the Wolf had him backed into the corner by the washing machine, the music of her voice hidden under wisps of steam. She was holding out his tea but he didn't look at it; his eyes were flaccid, watching her face. The air in the kitchen was thin, snapped taut and impossible to breathe. I retreated to the living room and turned the telly on. People talked on every channel, non-stop talking. Lying face-down on the floor, I realised how bad our carpet smelt, like a disease. The smell wiped out the sounds. I lay as still as poured concrete.

When I got up the light had gone and the smell of steak-and-kidney pudding pounded the walls like a trapped bird. She was standing in the middle of the kitchen, watching the potatoes boil. He was upstairs and I followed his tracks. Boots off by the shoe tidy, coat on the peg. Up the stairs – his bag open and spilling its guts onto their clean bed – and further down the passage to the bathroom. He was there, singing. I could hear him soaping up his hairy skin then rinsing, soaping and rinsing, still singing, his voice trapped by the cold, impenetrable tiles, its molecules silently ricocheting, infinite splitting atoms. Dividing and subdividing his precious noise until only fragments existed. The passage was cold and shadowed, with only one window that had a mass of spider plants reaching out and down to the floor. They stung on contact. I waited outside the door through his singing and soaping, rinsing and scrubbing. I listened to the bristles of the nailbrush digging out the dirt from his hands, the drag of the towel, and shut, shut of his deodorant spray. Various wafts of fragrance leeched out from under the door, mingling in the hall to concoct a scent-shadow of my dad – there he was before me in smell and behind the door for real. I was drenched in him. I would still try and resurrect him this way if I could, but it's impossible to get the concentration of perfumes right. And, besides, they don't make his brand of aftershave any more; it's obsolete, like him and me. I knew he would come out hungry and carry me downstairs, laughing, ready for dinner; but she called me to set the table and I couldn't wait for him.

We ate and dad told us jokes about French toilets and frogs' legs, but he hadn't eaten snails really and she told him to close his mouth while he chewed. I smiled until I ached and then dad took me up to bed and we looked for aeroplanes out the window. I curled into the hollow his weight had left in the flabby mattress and heard him coo at Mother downstairs, the shards of her reply piercing the floor. She followed her voice and arrived in my room: 'Want to sleep in mummy's bed tonight?'

Yes, yes, I nodded, nodded.

'You can come in later and let daddy think you had a nightmare, right?'

I stayed awake despite the bulk of exhaustion as they shut the house down and locked all the doors. She was first in their room, her teeth brushed and nightie on. I went in as planned, my eyes swollen against the light of the lamp and her face. I climbed into the middle between her and dad's empty space. 'Bad dream, treasure?' he said when he came in. Yes, I nodded, though it was a mesmerist's trick and not a truth, but the lights went off and I lay still, them breathing out of time with each other, her fast, him slow. I slept and I slept deep. No wolf that night. Dad was home and the lady skin stayed on.

Sunny days were happiest in our house. Mum and dad sat together and drank beer, and dad rubbed cream in lazy circles into her back while she read a magazine about fat women who married bad men over and over again and whose children had fatal illnesses. But that day it was raining and, because dad would be away working, we were going to buy my birthday present early so he could see my excitement and perhaps even my gratitude. Then we were going to have a little party with a cake. I wanted a bike. In the car, the windscreen wipers beat time in crotchets with the odd minim when the engine threatened to cut out, and mum was angry that we'd taken so long to get ready. My tooth brushing had been behind schedule, so the trousers that were too tight were wrenched up my legs. They itched and sounded like sand paper when they rubbed together at the tops of my thighs. Dad turned the radio on with a click. Puréed noises filled the car till he hit the right frequency and music filled in the gap their silence had left.

My bike was green with silver handlebars and a bell. I looked at it leaning against the house, absorbing and reflecting the sun. I wanted to touch it, get on it and ring the bell. But I didn't, not for a long time. It was so shiny and so perfect I didn't want to ruin it, cause scratches in the paintwork or get dirt embedded in the tyres. I didn't want anyone to touch it, not dad who wanted to tighten the brakes or Moira who came to look at it and have a go. I just wanted to look at it and dream of how I'd look riding it and how the earth would feel rolling under me. I belonged to it and it needed me. But I knew even then that the reality of my bike and I would disappoint. And I knew that all Wolfy did with her mesmerising was tart up an existence she never expected to claim. Mum and dad were in the kitchen getting my party ready. Their music spilled out of the house and I knew dad had chosen it to liven up the place, ready for when people came.

She was in the house reading wedding magazines, her long fingers stroking the pages of dresses and flower arrangements. My Nan said she shouldn't cry over might-have-beens and should live in the now. I fed the leftover birthday cake to the dog next door. Its long tongue curled itself around my fingers, fretting at each and every crumb of cake and pink icing. It waited only seconds for more then went off, its head low to the ground, searching. Dad had gone, too. My bike lay splayed on its side like a casualty in the grass. Within a few days the garden had almost digested it, its slow absorption gathering pace with the spring. The grass growing, consuming what you'd left and then, come winter and the grass's brittle decline, there it is, the thing you left and forgot, chewed up and rotten. Revealed. Bastard, bastard thing.

Moira and I went chasing demons up mountains and through forests of icy trees. We rode our bikes across the desert without stopping, the sun fat on our backs. Our blood getting thick and salty as a flat fish's from lack of water. We knew the ferocious tribe would have the map to the demon's lair; we just had to find them. Our magic bikes would find the way though, sniffing the trail and leading us on. None of it was real, obviously; it was just a game. Not a trick or lie, just a game. It was Moira's game. If I didn't want to do something or go where she said, she shouted and slapped and then finally cried real tears. So I did as I was told. But it was just a game; it wasn't real. The unreal was never easy to spot. That was a bad day. I had beetles running through my veins.

I had dinner at Moira's. We had to wait for her dad to come home before we could start, so we watched telly and the new baby with her brothers. The new baby was called David and his skin was perpetually damp. Everything he did seemed too much for him, breathing, shitting, sucking, and he looked as if he hated everyone. Perhaps he did; maybe he looked at us through his lizard eyes and saw ugliness, a milky haze of coagulated fat and blocked ducts. The baby was never quiet, even when not crying; when he sucked at his mum, he oozed sound. Noises just pitched out from him. Parents claim they can't wait for their baby to speak and say dada and choo-choo train, but that's a lie. The quickest thing children learn to do is shut up. Eat silently with your mouth closed, don't slurp, burp, or fart. Don't breathe through your mouth or suck your teeth or chew your lips when thinking. Don't try to suck up the juice of an apple when you take a big bite. And don't speak when the telly is on. Just shut the fuck up.

Dinner at Moira's came on lots of dishes. There was a dish for each separate food. Potatoes in one dish, sprouts in another, shepherd's pie uncut in a dish not a tin, gravy in a small jug and juice in a bigger one. Everyone served themselves without spilling, talking casually all the while. Moira's mum served me as I was the guest. I had something of everything. I thought they were extraordinarily posh.

We ate in the dining room; they had a dining room and a lounge. Separate rooms for separate things, no telly with dinner. The dad patted the mum on her knee under the table and she smiled back at him. Moira's brothers talked loudly. Her mum put the baby in his cot. Everyone ate.

'What did you little ladies do today?'

'Nicola smiled at Dirty Gerty.'

I had smiled at Dirty Gerty. I watched her as she left her busy house and walked toward me trailing whispers like a wedding veil. She was concocted from all the animals of the known world, her clothes and her hair, fish scales on her skin. She shone in the sunlight. She was clean like glass, honest clean, transparent clean. She smiled at me and I smiled back. She smelt like Margate, of candyfloss and salt and melting tarmac.

'You girls have been told not to speak to that woman, haven't you?' Her dad spoke with his mouth full, his cheeks red.

But we hadn't spoken, we'd just smiled. He knew that but he couldn't make us not smile at her or near her, so he pretended we'd spoken to her to justify his anger.

'Why not?'

'Because I say, kids, all right.'

'Why, what is she?'

'Does she steal kids and eat them?'

'She's just a bad lady who has too many friends.'

'Ah, let them be, Joe.'

Moira's mother turned to us and said, 'She sells solace to lonely hearts, kids, okay? She's not a witch or a kidnapper, just let the woman be now. Nicky, mummy says you are going to dance in the new show in town, you clever girl.'

I smiled, nodded and blushed, but I had no idea what she was talking about.

Jesus made miracles. Jesus could see me and he knew everything, and I believed when I died I would go to heaven and when my mother died she would go where the dead animals go because sweet baby Jesus knew.

I crossed the road by myself after dinner, trampling right through the mess of light from the street lamp. I was a shadow. The back door was open. I wiped the street from my shoes before going in. My mother lay on the sofa with her arms wrapped around a cushion. A record spun silently on the deck, the needle back in its cradle. She smiled at me and I went up to bed. The house folded in on us, neatly. I couldn't breathe in its modulated collapse. I got into bed, my nightie on back to front, with no good-night kiss. The sheets were cold like wet sand and clung to my bald skin. I left the curtains open. I saw high places through the window.

Sounds thrive even in silence. My bedroom crawled with minute swarms of breaths, sighs and footsteps. Being mute doesn't render you silent and being silent doesn't placate the ruckus. Nothing was wasted there. My body slowly filled up with hot oil and as it cooled and solidified I sunk head first, further and further like a sperm whale, deeper into the crushing pressure of sleep. My cavernous lungs containing enough stagnant oxygen to see me through, I knew better than to panic and watched placidly the sea of my unconscious. Past the currents and violent grabbing undertows, I saw clearly.

Finally there was silence.

The light couldn't reach in there but it wasn't dark. I watched my body make emergency repairs and patch-ups, layer cell upon cell. Atom by atom I grew. Taller and taller. That kind of sleep didn't permit gravity; it had rules that shirk the responsibilities of science. By morning, if I lasted that long, I could be a giantess. But someone would welsh on the deal. She would drag me to the surface and in my recovery from the bends I'd shrink back, like a soufflé brought from the oven too soon.

I woke to a dirty taste in my mouth and a smell of ancient skin. There was a feast going on, but not in my room. I heard the raucous clatter of a sumptuous eater; the smell festered in the air, drying my mouth with every breath. It robbed the atmosphere of moisture. The walls, the furniture, were as brittle as old bones. I got up to see, my feet and hands unruly with fear. I was trapped, rattling around in my body. My bedroom door opened with a rush under my hand; the oxygen sucked up, the hall vibrated, glowed incandescent. Through the heat haze I could see no fire — no fire but the heat was thick and slowing like sludge. My skin cracked, its fat spitting and sizzling, blisters burst on my hands and feet, and from Mother's bedroom came shrill voices and growls. The paint melted like wax from her door; it opened silently without my help. This was the feast, the party. She had a new victim. Still wearing her lady skin, she was huddled over him, cramming him in, moving so fast she was swallowing him whole, so fast there was no blood, no gore. He was pulling on her, grabbing at her, but he couldn't save himself. She was ramming him and mashing him up. Slamming and slapping at his flesh. She'd eaten so much I couldn't see where he began and she stopped. She made wet, sloppy noises as she chewed with her mouth open. I saw the black wolf hair between her legs. The curtains were drawn and pink flowers had burst open on the bed where she had changed the bedding. The dressing table and all her perfume bottles shuddered. But there was no blood. I crumpled under myself but, standing still, turned to escape.

Toast and a glass of squash. Green trousers. Mum smiling at me, the clammy weight of her false hand stroking my hair from my sweaty face. 'You look just like your dad this morning. One day, when you're a grown-up lady, you'll understand why secrets are better than hurting a person's feelings. Did you have another bad dream last night? You came in my room last night, didn't you? Yes, I know, I saw you. I was playing silly tickling games with Jeff, wasn't I? Mummy was lonely so Jeff came to keep me company. I get lonely when daddy goes away. No one to talk to or cuddle, eh? You won't talk to me, will you? So my pals come over to cheer me up, like you and Moira and your games. I get fed up with the telly and my magazines, Nicola, do you hear me, Nicola? Come on, Nic, look at me. Do you love me, sweetheart? Give mummy a kiss. Ah, that's nice! Keep mummy's secret, won't you, there's a good girl. Don't tell daddy about mummy's friends, will you, darling, eh, will you? Nic, don't tell daddy, will you? Bloody hell, Nic, look at me! Don't tell dad. Well then... don't just sit there like a spastic all the time, say something for fuck's sake, Nic. Jesus Christ, I didn't give birth to a bloody spastic, did I? Stop bloody gawping at me, Nikky. I know you can speak; I hear you up there. What is up with you, child? God, what the hell did I do to deserve this shit? I try my bloody best, don't I? I never beat you, do I? No. I'm not allowed a moment's peace, am I? Nothing for myself, nothing, just a pissing slave for you and your wanker father, ain't I? Eh? Do you know what? I wish you were both dead; I do. I could be me again instead of this. This isn't me, and this isn't my life: a loser husband and a dumb kid, in a poxy council house. Look at me, what did I do, eh? You, sitting there like a freak, sucking your fingers. Go on, go to school, you little cow. Get the fuck out of my sight — hurry up!'

I wished I'd been born without ears.

My grandfather had left his baccy tin on the kitchen counter, shiny like gold and smoothed by his calloused hands. He made his own skinny fags; shreds of tobacco dangled from the end, one side striped with spit to stick it together. His fags weren't neat like my mother's, boxed and ready-made like a microwave dinner. I prefer the scent of those scruffy fags even now. He would be missing his tin, and I wasn't surprised when he came through the front door. He was breathing so hard that his breath stained the air around him. He called my mum over and over, as if she were deaf. He didn't even say hello to me. Mum came in and he grabbed her arms, pulling her into our living room. I stayed still in the hallway, making sure I stayed on the plastic runner in the middle of our carpet; the carpet was new and I would get it dirty with my dirty, dirty feet. Even when I tried to stand completely still, I couldn't. My body was rowdy in the odd silence that punctured the house, my hands twitching and jolting, pre-empting command.

He drew an asbestos-roughened breath. I heard every thing he said to her. I knew they were sitting on the sofa because I'd heard the foam cushions exhale as they sat down. I knew that Granddad was going to say something terrible, and I knew that day would blacken like burning wood.

More people arrived, their bald faces metallic in the light. They crowded around my mum who sat on the sofa smoking a fag. They touched and spoke softly to her, the softness usually reserved for babies and the elderly. They gave her whisky for the shock and brandy to warm her up. Someone asked if she'd told me yet and she shook her head. She called me to her, her voice rusted by tears. I knew already what she was about to tell me; it wasn't a shock but still I tried not to hear. She pulled me to her body and held me there tight. She smelt like a wet dog. I could hear her heartbeat getting faster and faster, and suddenly I knew that she couldn't believe her luck.

'Nicky, daddy is dead. He smashed the lorry into a wall and his chest was crushed against the steering wheel. Your father is dead. Do you understand?' I nodded. I understood. He was dead and she couldn't believe her luck. Her excitement vibrated through me and she let me go.

Doctor Kennedy claims an experience of early grief is a determining factor in the construction of the self. It has also been said that the best and most functional of parents are dead ones. I choose to not decide which is right.

From then on there was always someone there with us, in the house. They made tea and brought pots of dinner to heat up, and listened to her wail and yell. She wore his clothes, replacing his precious skin cells and fragrance with her own foul wolfishness. I stole his slippers. The relatives helped her make decisions about what he should wear and the music she should have played and which readings were most suitable for a lorry driver, and I knew all she thought about was how to do her hair and what dress she should wear and how soon green trousers could move in.

I took his slippers behind my lavender bush and smelt him from his feet up. I put my hands inside them and, with my fingertips, felt the imprint of his feet, the shape of each toe, the height of his instep, the blunt ball of his heel. I traced the indent left by his private relationship with gravity. The terrible pain ripped at my throat; my chest froze solid. My dad had once taken me to the seaside; he carried me on his shoulders and bought me an ice cream, which melted quicker than I could eat it and dripped white stickiness onto the black of his hair. Now he had left me all alone. My throat was blocked by clots of sticky secrets. I was dying too.

Time melted, was a waxen pool at my feet. I couldn't remember what he looked like or the sound of his voice. She'd bleached him out of the house. The garden had turned inside out, showing its grisly innards. The grasses were drying in the thick winds. Moira and her brothers played in the street. They looked at me and waved but that was all.

She wouldn't get in the car. She was crying and crying, her face bloated like a sponge. That had to be her best trick yet. The constant crowd was silenced by her performance. She was a magnificent soloist. 'I can't go on without him, God, please no more!' We rode in the hearse, behind daddy lying in his box, his heart stabbed by one of his ribs. She had been humming to herself that morning, silly songs, and she couldn't even sing. They buried him very deep in the ground. He couldn't get out. She would get married again, to the green trouser man. She held my hand like it was a snotty tissue; she didn't want to hold it but knew she would need it later. No one paid attention to my dad; no one tried to rescue him; no one could see that she was a liar. The sky had pulled up its skirts, showing off its scanty Heliopause, and they didn't even see that.

There were too many people in the house, back for my dad's death party. They whispered very loudly, looking at my mum and then at me. Their papery bodies rustled against each other while they ate the sandwiches Nana Ada had made and drank the tea Aunt Joyce fermented in the kitchen. Somehow, even though this was my dad's big day, my mother was the centre of attention. Wailing and crying snotty tears, she was lying and lying. 'O, my darling man, how will I go on? Why, why, why did you leave me?'

And they believed her. They all believed her.

I stood on the edge of it all in my black frock, my black hair in funeral pigtails. The air was poisoned by her breath and I couldn't breathe. I was choking, my throat turning inside out, trying to purge the fumes and dredge up pure oxygen. They looked at me, even her, but they didn't help. No one thumped on my back or blew in my face. My eyes were melting. My larynx dilated and I puked all her filthy secrets over her clean carpet. I watched my voice, crusted with barnacles, pull itself up off the floor and tell the truth to all her lies. It took the centre spot effortlessly, so charismatic, creaking like her bed. Blood trickled out of my mouth from the crater my voice had left as it wrenched itself free, but I smiled, my teeth pink.

My voice ran around the room telling everyone the truth in one long sentence, and she couldn't catch it even though she chased, yelling, yelling. They were afraid of it, swatting it away like a fat spider. My clever voice didn't stop; it looked over its shoulder at me, winked, and told the lot. It told about green trouser man, about how she ate tongues, about how she tried to kill me every night, and how she wasn't a woman at all. Till fat Uncle Terry caught it and me, and threw us both into the garden.

I ran out through the gate into the street, my voice with me, and slowly, with inky feet, the pavement swallowing my footprints like words, I walked to Dirty Gerty's busy house. The small crowd of men parted and let me through to the front of the queue. I banged on her front door and the voice at my side shouted, 'Gerty, Gerty, open the cunting door.' Wonderful, chunky words, solid and indestructible, dolloped out and shaped with my tongue and teeth like marzipan.

She opened the door slowly, smiling as if she'd been expecting me, her silk gown ebbing and flowing over the riverbed of her body. The voice said, 'Why doesn't anyone like you? They call you Dirty Gerty and my mum said I must never talk to you.'

Gerty took me inside her house that smelt like candyfloss and burnt onions. All the curtains were drawn tight shut but every light was on. She sat on her orange velvet sofa and, handing me a strawberry lollipop, invited me to sit down. 'Surely,' she said, 'you know that no one likes an honest girl, especially one who fingers the liars. You can call me Lucy.'

I returned to live with my mother for a short time after that but, unaccustomed as she was to the shrill truth of my voice, I soon became too much for her. When her stomach started to pulse and throb with hers and Green Trouser's baby I was sent to live with my aunt. But even she couldn't take my voice and its digging underground with its white hands.

Now, much later, my nightmare has changed, and it was a nightmare – the staff here assure me that it was. She was never truly a wolf, they say, it isn't possible, and yet I am sure that she was. In the new dream I walk into my mother's bedroom in the middle of the night to find her sleeping, her human head on the pillow, mouth flaccid and leaking saliva, and her flesh loose around her chin. I pull back the covers and there is her wolf body: four legs, grey fur and humped chest. She still sleeps, unmoving. There are no sounds except for her snoring and occasional fart. In this dream I stand and watch my mother for hours till finally, as my flesh puckers with cold, I push a long carving knife into her chest and pull it down through her abdomen. The knife snags in her liver but with a sharp, sawing motion I finally cut right down to her doggy pelvis.

I reach into the soggy tear and yank out armfuls of hot, slippery intestines, steaming kidneys and a piss-full bladder. I pull out everything till she is clean, leaving a neat pile of her indelicate offal by the side of her bed. Tucking my chin to my knees, I roll inside the dry cavity of her body and, wearing her wolfy body, I finally sleep.

Smokin'
the Queen

by Kay Sexton

'The thing is, I cyaan' do it.' Darius heard how much he'd changed in the words he spoke. He'd said 'thing' rather than the true Jamaican 't'ing', but the long 'a' and missing 't' in 'cyaan'' were pure Jamdown and the heavyweight 'it' that finished the sentence slammed down like a machete.

He didn't want to know so much. Self-understanding was the goal of rehab, but once he'd got it, there seemed no getting rid of it. It sat on his shoulder and told him about himself. It made him look at the world straight on. So he knew he'd changed how he sounded because of spending time with the Pastor, and if he went back down into Tooting now, his old voice would return. But he knew also that the way he spoke was a lie. On the streets he'd call it Jamaican, but how could it be when the island-born Pastor said 'thing' and 'problem' but London-born Darius said 't'ing' and 'prablaam'?

People lived in lies. They wrapped themselves in Babylon until it filled their hands and eyes and mouths and they suffocated on it.

'... problem.' He heard the Pastor say.

Darius nodded to keep the man happy. Self-awareness was ruining him. Three nights ago he'd got drunk after his set — not just drunk, but really red. And when the warm Brixton air had reached him, ripe with beer and patties, cheap scent and coconut hair oil, he'd leaned against the wall, fighting the nausea chewing on his gut. It wasn't until he was in the taxi on the way home, deck beside him, LPs in two cases in the foot-well, that he realised he'd become old. Self-awareness told him so. He saw himself leaning against the wall, one hand holding his belly, the other pressed against sheeny red brick. A young man would have been on the ground – legs bent, head rolled back – but an old man feared he wouldn't get up again once he was down. An old man would inch along the wall, walking on the outside of his feet, bending over if he had to, but locking his knees so he couldn't fall. And that was how Darius had seen himself.

Once the badness passed he'd straightened up and made sure he strode out of the alley, but he'd seen his future there: a pork pie hat, grizzled white hair, church twice a week. Dominoes and past glories would be his entire conversation and he would step aside for young men in the street.

He'd nearly asked the driver to turn round and take him back to Kennington where he could connect. Instead he pressed his hands hard between his knees until his fingers were yellow and grey. When he looked up from mashing his hands the cab was at his front door. He carried the deck and records into the house, and made hot chocolate the way his mother had, putting it back on the hob once he'd mixed the cocoa with the brown sugar and water, and boiling it again with grated nutmeg before stirring in condensed milk. He sat down on his chair and relived the evening in his head, running through the tracks he'd played and the crowd's reaction. Cecil's empty chair faced his and he'd been able to imagine he was telling Cec-mon about the set. Except it was too cold and too quiet.

He'd switched on the electric heater and then looked along Cecil's shelves for the right record. Cab Calloway, he'd decided. He chose a CD, the 1945 original with Milt Hinton on bass - not as good as the 1942 pressing of *Nagasaki*, but he'd sold that to help pay for Cecil's funeral. He remembered the one time Cecil had played it for him – the background hiss would have filled this emptiness. He'd sat back down, warming his hands on the chocolate tea, to tell a dead man about the night's events.

'... has to be done,' said the Pastor.

Darius frowned. 'I don' see why.'

'How long have you been living in Cecil's house?' asked the Pastor.

'T'ree mont' maybe?' Darius knew he was reacting to the other man's clear diction by playing up his own, but he didn't seem able to stop, just as he couldn't stop the frenzied jiggling of his right foot, which danced like the vestry floor was too hot to touch. 'You know, some places, they'd say I got the devil in my foot to be doing that,' he observed.

The Pastor sighed. 'Don't change the subject, Darius. Cecil's house has to be cleared out. Shall we start tomorrow?'

Darius felt heat rising through his clenched teeth to bug out his eyes.

'You don' respect me,' he began. He watched his foot, toe planted, heel bouncing. Its arrhythmic movement demanded order, a pattern to impose on chaos. He cycled music in his mind, choosing and rejecting, until he found the opening bars of Duke Ellington's *Caravan*; the plosive drums like empty bottles spinning on a dance floor, the contrapuntal piano insisting on being heard without joining the melody. No harmony, just sounds bouncing, ricocheting off each other until the bass skinned them together. It worked. His foot took the beat and settled into it. When he looked up again the Pastor was watching him with patient incomprehension.

Darius had tamed the chaos, but there was nothing left over for manners. 'It's not Cecil's house.' The jazz came to bolster him like a friend at his shoulder in a confrontation. 'T'ree mont' now and you act like I squattin'. It my house now.'

The Pastor held up his hand, but Darius let the music take him up and over the gesture, standing, stretching, bracing his arms on the other man's desk, pushing hot eyes into the other man's face. 'What you t'inkin'? You t'ink I trick the old man, or frighten him into leavin' me his place?'

The Pastor tried to speak but Darius slapped both hands down on the wood, letting the jinking notes of Ellington's piano flurry around the flat bang. 'My house! My house!' he heard himself shouting and threw his disordered body back into the chair.

'You act like a bad man, Darius. You know you're going to get trouble that way.' The Pastor sighed, like a sigh was his jag. 'I understand your crosses. Why not ease up? Take a holiday.'

Darius hardly took in what he was saying. The erratic beat of *Caravan* had segued into Capelton's *Almshouse* and it was difficult to hold himself in the conversation. What did it matter? Nothing mattered. The world had become a series of truths he didn't care to know and couldn't stop himself from seeing. Being straight was like a prison you signed yourself into after you'd been your own judge and jury. A life sentence. All he could do was find distractions to give him ten minutes, five minutes, two minutes away from self-awareness. He had to remember, too, that he'd lived in this world before skunk rearranged his mind and got him committed. This was reality. It was all he was going to get.

'You feel downpressed by the death of your friend. It's natural. I think you should go to where he grew up — pay respects to him, maybe find his people. Give thanks.' The Pastor never stopped his chatty chatty. Darius wove it into the music and nodded in time to the beat. 'You know there are things in there belong to other people? Darius?'

He nodded.

'Then you know why we have to find things — the cello he's left to his school, the records he wants donated for auction...'

The Pastor's voice faded away and Darius filled his head with sound. It was *Life After Death* by Natas, mixed with *For no reason at all in C* by the late, great, died-before-his-prime Bix Beiderbecke. There was another sound too, the hiss of rain. He closed his eyes and was back there, mixing the tunes for Cecil's funeral, a proper jazzman's funeral — with music. He'd hired a float from the Brixton Carnival, just to get decks with enough sound, and from his high vantage point he'd been able to see the front gates where Jamaicans had turned out to their steps to mark Cecil's passing. From a couple of houses came old men carrying beat-up saxophones or banjos, joining the walking wake. Many of them had been people from his mother's church. Darius had known them since he was a bare-arsed picanniny and they raised their chins to him, to tell him that he had a debt to pay now — if they honoured the old man, he should come and honour them, Sundays, in church. But some were just people that must have known Cecil when he was a jazzman, a middle-rank player in the old, old days.

They'd been an ugly collection — fat men and skinny, all elderly or outright old, red noses and purple lips, grizzled grey hair on the black men, pale shining scalps on the white combo members. Old, old, men. He was lost in a world of old men.

He opened his eyes to find the Pastor staring at him. 'Sure t'ing,' Darius said, fastening his coat and heading out into the night. Heading home.

It wasn't really his home, just his house. He had grown up next door, in the house where his mother had died. The council had refused to let him stay on — citing his drug treatment and psychosis as reasons for putting him in sheltered housing. He'd had twenty-eight days to move, and on the twenty-third Cecil died. He'd been an old man, old enough to fight in the Second World War; Darius had no need to feel shame, but he did. The jibber-jabber in his head told him that he'd ill-wished the old man for his house, even though the inheritance had surprised everyone, Darius most of all. That was why he needed the music, to shut out the jibber-jabber.

Three days later he found Cecil's house, his house, had been invaded. He came home from Soul Kitchen with two steaming chicken patties and a large woman in a blue nylon button-through overall refused to allow him into his own, Cecil's own, kitchen.

'I don't care if you're the Lord a Heaven in a flamin' chariot!' she bellowed. 'This kitchen's a disgrace and no yout's goin' to come and tell me my bidness.'

He sat on the front step, trying to work out whether this was inside his head or outside. A fat grandmother giving him orders in his own house? Didn't seem like a skunk thing. But before, when his head had crawled with things, it was often the small things that tripped him up, pissed him off until he was raving and punching air that had gelled around him into the form of his worst tormentors. He was clean, so clean he squeaked, but before he'd been clean too and the things had still gibbered at him, lurking in the ticket barriers at Tooting Bec station, swinging from the rear-view mirrors in taxis, strap-hanging in the aisle of the number 270 bus, until the only safe place was the tiled height of the underground tunnels where the things seemed unable to follow him.

The Babylon doctor had said Darius was a danger to himself and others. Nobody had argued with him, not even Darius's mother, who'd had to watch him being loaded into a police van after he'd 'run amok' in Tooting Broadway. He couldn't remember any of it — except sometimes he'd meet somebody who'd been in the street that day, and he'd see in their faces that he'd been running and he'd been amok, whatever that meant. It seemed to mean involuntary committal, and scars on his arms and skull, long pale worm tracks from the glass he'd smashed in the shop windows. His mother had told him it meant his last, last chance was right under his nose and if he messed up this time, she wouldn't be able to take him home again. What he knew for sure was running amok meant he'd been left with two choices — saying no to skunk or saying yes. And while it was like that, it was simple enough. Every day was an uphill climb from opening his eyes to sinking to sleep, and on that climb he said 'nah, mon' to every risk and seduction: no rum, no parties, no skinning up, no skunk, not even any grass, no pretty girls who might lead him into temptation. And it had been easy easy because while he was serving his forty days and nights in rehab, his mother had died. They said it was a stroke but he knew he'd broken her heart. He'd come home to an empty house, the Pastor had told him things he'd ignored, and he'd sunk into something else. Dreamland. Not the *Dreamland* sweetness of Thelonious Monk — it had been just a place where he got through his days on Eminem and Tupac and his nights had been filled with Tylenol he bought on the street.

Cecil had changed all that. At first he was just the old white man who'd been next door as long as Darius could remember. He'd used to play records when Darius was a kid, classical music he knew now, but back then it had just been sounds that went with the strangeness of him, the whiteness, the oldness. Darius's mother had always sniffed when his name was mentioned, but it had been more dismissive than insulting — like Cecil was some kind of dutty old dog living in the yard and to be tolerated.

He was the only white in the street when Darius was a child. By the time he was teenaged, there were a few white couples moving in, and some white women with black men, and many Pakistanis and Ugandan Asians whose parents lived in Bradford or Manchester but who had moved down to London for jobs, or to get away from their families. And Cecil. He'd stopped going out much in his sixties, and then the women in the street would sometimes call on him, banging on his door like the second coming, handing him a covered bowl and telling him about their charity like it was a vice. 'We had plenty rice and peas at the church tonight, so I thought you could use up a bowl for us, Mister.'

Cecil in his shirt sleeves, more courtly the older he got. 'Thank you — I appreciate the thought and the food. I've a great fondness for peas and rice.' And the woman would bounce back down the path, cutting her eyes right and left as if daring anybody to see her as a good Samaritan.

Then Cecil was older still and Darius forgot about him, till he banged on the wall with his walking stick and, when Darius got round there, sat him down in the tall wooden-legged chair Darius still used, and asked him about Ragga.

At first Darius thought he was hearing things. 'You dissin' me, mon?'

Cecil had given him a pale stare and held up his shaking hands to show the record he was trying to fit onto an old turntable.

Darius skootched forward off the chair and on to his haunches when he saw the old man's prize, The Wailing Wailers — it couldn't be one of the first pressings from 1966. It couldn't be. It was.

They'd listened in a silence more hostile than respectful. Marley filled the world and Darius looked at the skin and bones opposite him and tried not to smile.

'Where you get that?' Darius challenged.

'Bought it when it came out, like everybody else.' The milk-eyed glare was steady but the hands weren't. 'Sleeve it for me please, Darius.'

He hadn't gone home for five hours. Long past the time the old man must have been aching in his joints and dying for his bed, Darius had prowled the record shelves, pulling down vinyl, exclaiming over things he'd heard about, but never heard, and waiting each time for the old man's nod before setting the disc on the turntable and falling back into the chair to listen.

If it had been just pity, it wouldn't have worked. But Cecil wanted to know about Ragga. He insisted Darius bring round a CD player and take him through the history of the fusion movement and explain how Asian dub and bhangra fitted into the picture. Where Darius didn't have the right tracks, the seminal sounds showing the evolution of the music, Cecil sent him down to HMV to buy them.

In return Cecil played him jazz. He learned the strange, short tale of Bix Beiederbecke and the long love affair between black men and the saxophone. He found the Count and the Duke and Bird and the Trane as though they'd been waiting for him all along, just a little way behind the things skunk had pulled from his head. He felt Art Blackey's beat like an uncle's blessing and his playing like an old friend's smile. He picked up with Davis and Monk and let Ella and Cab sing him to sleep. Without knowing how it happened, he began to make a place in the world again — a small perimeter patrolled by music, within which he was safe and could let down his defences.

Cecil took to Raggamuffin big time. He was crazy mad for bhangra beats. Night after night Darius was banging on the wall to stop the old man running tracks through his newly acquired boom box until dawn. One night he'd laughed out loud — what was the world coming to? The crazy black bwoy was telling old whitey to hush up the rap so he could get some sleep. He'd rolled over and then found himself shivering and shaking, rocking on his haunches with tears dripping off his chin, and he could mourn the woman who'd died and gone into the ground while he was still in a psychotic haze.

The old man must have heard through the wall. The next day he said, 'Your mother was a good woman, a brave woman.' Darius gave him a hot look, which was all that passed between them on the subject.

Eventually Darius found the cello. And he only had to look at it once, where it stood inside the wardrobe, to know.

'Hellfire mon! You the maas!' He charged downstairs and over to the shelves, pulling out the LP with the colour cover showing the quintet with Cecil at the back, almost hidden behind his instrument. Darius would never have recognised him, but the cello he knew at first glance, its unusual red colour and rich patterning were distinctive.

'Mon, you played with the Trane!' Then, turning, seeing the old man's stern misery, he looked again at the shaking hands and realised he was facing something bigger than he'd thought. He sank to the ground, cradling the record, gazing into the faces – all dead except the one white one, the one he had been living next to for his whole life without knowing it. There was no way to conceal his shame at his ignorance. 'Maas,' he said again. 'You one devious old man, you know that? I should be shinin' you shoes for you' talent.'

Cecil had shaken his head, but he'd smiled.

That was why Darius became a DJ. Not a rapper, but a mixer of tracks. And not so much because of Cecil, but because they were his family, his people: Bird, Trane, Monk and all the rest, and this Babylon land hadn't told him. So he told them. He mixed *Boplicity* with *Yellow Brick Road* and let Miles and Eminem duke it out. He ripped *My Favourite Things* into *Over Here* and the club went wild. The music didn't fill the holes in his head, more like it pulled them into crazy shapes that took away the fear, made them into contortions of terror, – like Disney versions of horror stories. He wasn't holding it together; he was controlling the way it fell apart.

Cecil had always been there, with something in his hands: a crinkled sleeve round a heavy black disc that chucked music out like a missile, smashing into his brain, hacking down his understanding of the world so he had to rebuild it again around the knowledge that Paul Robeson was a tortured man with a voice of brass and honey, Billie Holliday's like would never be seen again, for vocal power or talent abused, that when Darius's grandfather came to Britain there were television shows where white men wore black faces to serenade white women. Darius didn't care, didn't even judge; that's what the holes were for, he'd decided, to make room for all the weirdness of reality. Cecil always there, but known for less than a month, old man's hands, shaking and cold, old man's memories, a war, a love of jazz, a lost generation. Cecil who'd fallen asleep one night and never woken up. Cecil who'd left Darius his house and his legacy. Cecil.

Darius let his head crank round by small degrees until he was staring up at his own front door, wedged open, wafting the harsh perfumes of scouring powder and detergent. Skunk demons didn't ever come with hygiene, no fuckin' way. He picked up his patties and walked past his mother's house — now let out by the council to a family from Bosnia — down to the church.

'I thought we agreed, Darius,' said the Pastor. 'We need to find everything Cecil's included in his bequests to meet his wishes. We need to move out all of Cecil's clothes. It's time to make the place your own.'

That was what he didn't need. Take away Cecil and what was left? Crazy, skinny black man with a house he didn't know how to live in and holes in his head. Turn Cecil into a duppy instead of a presence still in the room, in the chair, in the music, and Darius was lost. Lost.

But then, he was lost if he told them he couldn't cope without Cecil's spirit filling the place with the smells of carbolic and cocoa and those freaked-out striped mints he called humbugs, tasting of soap and toothpaste. They'd lock him up again, certain sure, if he admitted that Cecil's presence pulled him through the days, and that the only way he knew to live was to swan-dive towards Cecil's aged fragility and hope the intervening years got out of the way.

So he nodded without smiling and let the Pastor lead him home and introduce him to Morrie and Annie, women who'd known his mother and clipped his ear when he was a child, but who'd fallen through one of the holes in his skunk time. And they showed him a sparkling kitchen and told him next they'd tackle the bedrooms. He thought about the cello like a corpse in the wardrobe and his panic must have shown because the Pastor took him back to the church again, and gave him a bed for the night before repeating the idea of a holiday. And Darius nodded without smiling.

Two days later he was hugging Cecil's cello case on Streatham station. The Pastor had panicked about the long journey and it had been Darius's rare pleasure to calm him down. 'Mon, don' worry. When I's pickney I spen' half my time on trains – I an' I been from Mitcham to Mill Hill and Beacontree to Gunsbee. The brethren did swim and clumb trees 'til the park man done stop us. Don' fear, I can do this t'ing.'

'Gunsbee?' the Pastor had queried, staring at Darius clutching the hard case like a fat woman's coffin.

'Gunnersbury.' Darius handed out all four syllables.

'Ah, yes. But Dorset is still a long way away...'

Darius shrugged.

'Fine. I'm glad you're willing to take this on. The cello was obviously important to Cecil and returning it to his school seems an appropriate thing for you to do. It honours his name.'

Darius shrugged again. He could have told the Pastor this cello wasn't being returned anywhere; it had never belonged to a church school, not with that amazing red inlay; it was a jazz cello, made for clubs and bars. But it wasn't his problem. Cecil wanted to give a cello to his school, fine – let them have it. Not his business. His problem was he had only a little while left before Cecil disappeared from the house under the women's scouring and airing. So perhaps it would be better to be away for a few days, like a reprieve, before facing his psychosis.

'Remember the records,' he cautioned the Pastor, who nodded. 'And the chairs. Don't take the rugs. I wan' keep the magazines too...'

'I promise you, Darius, when you get back the front room will be just as you left it. We'll clean but that's all. Not a thing will be taken from that room.'

Darius snorted. Something would be taken. Cecil would be gone.

The train was sleek, like a shining maggot. Darius gave it a long look – Babylon. But he got on board with the cello and his sports bag and nodded to the Pastor.

After the train pulled away he rummaged through the bag, checking his CDs and player. He could have had an iPod or MP3, but he didn't trust them. They were like voices in his head. CDs he could manage. They were real, you could fuck them up: scratch them, sit on them. Anything you could fuck up he could cope with.

The second train was better. An old, faded thing, with slam doors and overhead racks made of string, like fishing nets. He sat in the middle of the carriage, resting his cheek on the cello case and watching the dust rising from the seats to waltz in the heat from the scratched and smeary windows. He drowsed. The rhythm was pure ska and the musty odour of upholstery and a hundred thousand journeys was comforting. It was like Cecil.

The station was small and throttled by greenery. He'd hoped for a cab rank outside, but there was nothing and when he went back in the pale grey man behind the slatted glass pointed to the payphone. Darius rang the number on the card tucked behind the mounting. He had some difficulty getting the dispatcher to understand him, but eventually he arranged for a car to drive him to St Cecilia's. He waited outside for half an hour but no cab appeared. When he went back to the phone the dispatcher hung up on him. The grey man smiled, thinning his lips. Darius felt his eyes begin to burn and heat rising up in his throat. The grey man beckoned him over.

'Did she put the telephone down on you?' he asked, his voice over-ripe with rolling sounds that made Darius think of fat, purring cats. He nodded, not trusting his superheated temper.

'Ah... well, she's not always in the right mood for strangers. If you can hold on twenty minutes or so, the school minibus will be arriving and they'll take you right to St Cecilia's, which will save you quite a sum of money from the taxi, don't you think?'

Darius didn't see there was a choice. He could have asked if the woman hung up on all her customers or just black-sounding ones, but he wasn't sure he would get an answer, or like it if he did.

He crouched on the kerb with the cello between his knees until the ancient green bus arrived, then sat in front, near the driver, with seventeen pairs of eyes drilling into his back. Most of the eyes were young – the students, he guessed – but there were one or two tweedy men who might be teachers.

The college was small and ugly. The man he had come to meet was small and ugly. Darius didn't want to hand the cello to him. The caressing way he took the case was obscene and Darius looked away.

'Cecil was a good cellist,' the little man stated as he peered at the cello front and back and hefted its weight.

'He was a great mon, great cellist,' Darius insisted. 'A maas.'

'A master? Oh, I don't think I could go that far. And history judges more harshly even than I do. Of course, if he'd stuck to his last, followed through on his early promise...'

Darius glared.

The little man flinched but continued. 'I know what your people think. And Cecil was a great... supporter of, well I suppose you could call it negro music, couldn't you?'

'What you mean?' Darius felt himself beginning to shake with fury.

'Well, he was mixed up with that woman... until he met her jazz was just a pastime for him, but after he met Sugar Brown, well...'

'I don' know what you're talkin' 'bout.' Darius let the heat in his voice emerge.

'Oh well, I'm sure you can't be expected to understand. You're probably related, aren't you?'

Darius stared at the cello.

The man misunderstood. 'Yes, lovely, isn't it? He must have been playing it until the very last days of his life.'

'I don' know what you talkin' 'bout,' Darius said again. 'Cec-mon never play that cello. I live nex' door all my life, and never heard it.'

'Well, that's as may be, but this cello is seasoned to the hand; it's alive. The tone is good and the wood has been handled regularly. It takes up the warmth of the body, you know, and the oils of the skin.'

Darius thought back to Cecil's 'siesta' every afternoon, a habit he said he'd picked up during the war when he'd served in Italy. He imagined the old man, sitting silent in his room, keeping the cello alive without playing it. 'So what?'

'So maybe he regretted sacrificing his classical career?'

Darius was back-tracking the conversation. 'Who's Sugar Brown?'

The little man showed his teeth in a tombstone smile. 'Don't you know about Sugar... and the other one? Alice, her name was. Oh dear, and there I was thinking you were some kind of relative.' He looked like the quarrelsome dogs old white men owned: low to the ground with sour pink rims to their eyes and pale gums from which the lips receded in a snarl whenever they saw Darius. Dogs that could smell illness and attacked it.

Darius waited for the rest of the story, sure the man would tell it because harm was his objective.

'Well now, Sugar Brown can't have been her real name, she was probably called Doris Smith or something, and she was an American... black person. She had some pretensions to being a singer, but everybody knew she was a floozy — there was a rather unsavoury man, some kind of South American I think, who kept her. She turned up in England a couple of times, probably because she wasn't good enough to make a go of a singing career in America. By all accounts, Cecil was besotted with her, helped her cut a record, although nothing ever came of it. Anyway, hanging around with a... a second-rate singer effectively ended his orchestral prospects. And then, not long after he'd thrown his chances away, she went back to the US of A — I did hear tell the man who kept her made her go back, though I can't swear to the truth of that — and Cecil ended up living with the woman who'd been her maid. Alice her name was. Very sad.' He didn't look sad, more as though he was waiting to see the outcome of a nasty practical joke.

'You only telling me Cecil had a woman?'

'Well, not just any woman. I mean both women were... well, like you.'

'Black,' Darius stated it.

'Mmmm.' The small man seemed to recognise he might have misjudged his audience. 'Of course, there's nothing wrong with that, nothing at all, or not now anyway, but back then... and especially after the girl died.'

'She died?'

'Mmmm... soon after she went back to America. Drugs overdose. Nothing at all to do with Cecil of course, but people always wondered, afterwards, if he... you know.'

Darius shook his head, although he knew damn fine how people thought and what they wondered.

'Whether he took drugs,' the small man hissed conspiratorially.

Darius leaned forward. 'You never met Cecil, did you?' He asked it low and quiet, as though sharing a secret.

'No, sadly not. He was a friend of my father's though.' He stuck out his lips like a child denied a sweet.

Darius leaned even further, offering the intimacy of gossip. The other man craned his neck forward as though expecting Darius to whisper straight into his ear.

'Cecil was a good man, and you should wash out your dutty mouth,' Darius murmured.

The man blinked. Darius stood, letting himself loom and tower. It felt good to frighten the nasty little creature.

It wasn't until he got outside that he remembered the pig was supposed to be fixing a place for him to stay. He walked back along the broken tarmac road. It wasn't bad to get around without the cello to slow him down. He patted the pocket with his return ticket. He could go back whenever he wanted, as long as he was ready to watch the disintegration of his home. When he reached the main road he looked left and right. Left led to the station eventually. To the right, around a bend in the road, he could see a pub sign. He wanted time to think.

The pub was like a roadhouse, painted red and yellow. It was more garish and familiar than he'd been expecting – his television-filled childhood had led him to think all country pubs were thatched and oak-beamed – but its tacky, standardised exterior was misleading. Inside it was rural, and old-fashioned enough for all conversation to stop as he entered. He ordered lager and stood at the bar, watching his own face in the mirror as he drank fast.

Cec-mon had been living with a black woman. That made sense of the women who'd fed him; they might not admire his colour but they'd have respected the power of his heart. And so Cecil had been a real dog after all! He'd followed after some smoky girl in a high-slashed dress with a good set of pipes. So how come he'd ended up living with her maid? But then, Cec was a waste-not-want-not man. Maybe he and Alice had been thrown together when Sugar went home. Darius was never going to know; nobody would tell him now, and anyway that wasn't his business. He smiled, for Cecil in a warm bed with a warm body – the sly old rogue.

He'd almost finished the pint before he realised that what he'd taken for other customers were two life-sized mannequins. They sat at a table: Bruce Lee on one side, arms akimbo, Stan Laurel on the other, scratching his head. There was only one real customer, a tiny old man who looked half-asleep.

Darius put down the glass, turning on his heel to examine the effigies. They were repellent, vivid and as out of place as he was. The man behind the bar leaned forward to swab at the surfaces. 'Gave you a start, did they?'

Darius had no idea what the man meant; the words had to be taken apart and rebuilt before he could understand anything these people said. Then he nodded.

'A real conversation point, they are. I can't tell you how many strangers have got the surprise of their lives when they realised they were supping up with Stan and Bruce there. The Lee brothers I call them: Stan-lee and Bruce Lee, see?'

'Three,' said a woman's voice.

Darius turned again, to see her against the gauzy light of afternoon through the dusty windows.

'Not with you, Mel.' The man behind the bar had gone back to his mopping, but his down-turned face jutted across the bar top like an invitation to fight.

'Including...' She smiled, extending her glass towards Darius in acknowledgement.

'Darius,' he said.

'Including Darius.' She lowered her glass and smiled into it, as though sharing a secret with its emptiness. 'Exactly three strangers in two years have had the surprise of their lives as a result of your big dolls there.' She cocked the glass towards the Lee brothers. 'Another half please.' The glass came to rest silently on the bar. 'And one for yourself.'

Her voice was low and deep. She'd sing contralto, Darius decided, and as she stepped closer to him he picked up the sweetness of her smell and the way the light danced in the corkscrewed ends of her caramel hair. 'And one for Darius.' Her smile ripened and he felt the tightening of sexual interest in her sidelong glance, which took in the sticky bar, the sulking barman and Darius himself, from his belt buckle down, in a direct assessment as uncomplicated as sex had felt – until he'd learned to fear his madness would resurface through his pleasure and tip him into a devilish place.

'We're in the beer garden, Darius...' Her voice floated back as he watched her vanish into the darkness beyond the bar. Her long, dark skirt receded most completely, then her mass of hair. Finally the horizontal bands of her T-shirt faded into the gloom, leaving behind the sweet tang of her perfume.

Darius found he had drunk the whole of his second pint in the few moments between her words and her disappearance, so he ordered another half and carried it with her refilled glass into the dark warmth beyond the bar. His hands shook and he felt ahead with his toes, seeing the white gleam of his trainers like blind fish swimming upstream. He heard the barman behind him: one word – it could have been bitch, or witch.

The dark corridor led to a walled yard, a scanty waste with broken tables and umbrellas with bent spokes. Half a dozen men sprawled across a pool table or crouched around its base, watching two men wrestling. One was blond, the other dark, both wore sweat-marked T-shirts and jeans. A corrugated plastic roof threw orange and grey shadows across the torn baize and the faces of the watchers. Darius paused, balanced between dark and light, feeling the stickiness of the lino under his feet and the cool slickness of the glasses in his hands. Vertigo blurted him out into the sun, cold sweat inching down his spine in a panic against the loss of self racing towards him.

The girl, Mel, had circled round the wrestlers to lean against the brick wall. Darius fixed his eyes on her and each step he took was easier than the last. By the time she took her glass from him, he was steady enough to smile.

'Do you fancy your chances?' She angled one rounded shoulder towards the wrestlers. He knew it was flirtation, but chose to respond seriously. He lowered his head to scrutinise the two men who had hold of each other's waists and were each trying to gain enough purchase to throw the other.

'Looks dangerous to me,' he said.

'Most things are dangerous, if you come down to it.'

He inspected her answer and decided he didn't have a reply he wanted to make. One wrestler, the yellow-headed one, lifted the other a couple of inches from the ground. Roaring, he blundered forwards, shoving his opponent into scattering watchers.

Darius looked away.

Mel touched him and he felt his skin shiver like a horse's hide, each pore trying to recoil and move towards her simultaneously. He glanced down. Her hand looked like a pale flower, the kind a man would tuck in his buttonhole in an old movie. He could imagine doing it. It made him smile.

He let himself look at her. Eyes like Cec-mon's, blue and not soft. Fair, fine skin that looked like it would stay dented if he pressed it. If he thought about putting his mouth to her neck, he could imagine the pressure of his lips would show on her forever. A wide mouth, wide shoulders, haunches like a black girl, velvety curves not pin-sticky hip bones like a lot of white women. A good looker, no doubting it. But it was her voice that was bending him out of shape – a milk and honey voice, a Promised Land voice. Every word she said was a blessing.

She smiled and he looked down into his glass.

The blond wrestler made a feint, swinging right to put his opponent off balance and then lunging hard to the left, his shoulder hitting the other man's midriff. Air whooshed over his head as he pushed, pushed, driving the man backwards. The crowd around the pool table scattered as the two locked bodies crashed into it and then the feinter lifted, tipped, and his rival was sprawled on the table.

The watchers cheered and jeered and the victor performed a little huffing dance, a clumsy victory step.

'What does he win?' Darius asked.

'He just wins,' Mel replied.

Three hours later the pub doors had been closed. 'Old Mike, he doesn't like our company, but he's too mean to say no to our money, so we drinks out here and when we're ready we leaves by the wall,' Bran said.

Bran was the winning wrestler and somehow he'd struck up the idea that Darius had been on his side.

'So the landlord locks you out the pub? Mon, that's Babylon,' Darius said.

'Don't know about that, but Mike's is the only place in walking distance, see. We don't like him more than he likes us; we just put up with each other, like.'

'You're not from here, are you?' Darius asked. Bran's speech was as peculiar as the station guard's, but different.

'I'm Welsh, mate! My Da came here to work on the sheep and never went back. Married local first though, so my Ma's from the Valleys too.'

Darius nodded. He had no idea what it all meant, but Bran kept offering him a two-litre bottle of cider. He would drink the blood-warm contents and pass it to Mel without looking at her. He didn't need to look. He could feel her body against his, softer but more solid, her curves pressed against him from hip to shoulder. He heard her each time she drank, soft noises like midnight dreams, and the gentle intimacy of her sigh as she wiped her mouth before handing the bottle back to him. It was like a song, a wordless threnody. He was feeling no pain, that was for sure.

It wasn't just cider in there, he knew that. There was something sweeter and stronger, like fruit ripe with alcohol. He didn't care to know what. Bran talked continuously, quietly, like a man who would stop breathing if his voice ran out. Darius hadn't understood a word he'd said in the last hour but now, with the descending heat of the booze, and the sun hot on his head, he thought he was beginning to pick out the sense of it again.

They were watching a skinny youth building a tower with beer mats. It kept falling, because of the uneven ground, because the youth's gangling limbs knocked into it, because other drinkers flicked pebbles at it. He'd been working on it for an hour or more. Darius didn't mind. He gazed at the construction. The shadows moved, orange became grey, grey became mauve. The bottle had to be tipped higher and sounded a lighter, emptier note with every swig.

'Bus!' An urgent voice from behind them blurted the word like a warning. People began to rise and brush themselves off, groaning and chuckling, excavating pockets and counting coins. Darius watched as each figure climbed the pile of empty beer barrels and stepped over the rear wall of the garden. Mel stood, Darius stood, and Bran fell, still clutching the bottle. Liquid foamed across the baize and sank like a green tide. Mel pushed back her hair, sighed and climbed the barrels. At the top of the wall, silhouetted by the sun, she paused. 'Come on, Darius,' she said.

He turned back to the table. Bran snored like an old man, uneven, vague, as though it hurt. Darius sighed before bending to pull Bran's body from the baize, propping it against one of the table legs where it slid to the ground. He frowned.

'Darius, leave him.' Her voice held no impatience, but it was still an order.

He shrugged, with his back to her. 'I no can do that. He could t'row up and die like this.' He looked away as she stepped over the wall and disappeared.

He lugged Bran upright again, and propped him with one hand while looking around for a way out. The pub door was closed, and he could bet it would be locked.

He grabbed an empty half-barrel and stood it between Bran's legs, wrapping the man's arms around it and resting his head on the metal rim. It wasn't a guarantee but if the drunk did throw up, it would help. Not enough though. He looked at his jacket. He didn't need it. Even if he had to sleep out, he would be warm enough tonight. He wadded the jacket and jammed it behind Bran's head to prevent it rolling.

There was a sound on the wall and the gawky mat-piler reappeared. 'You've missed the bus,' he said.

Darius straightened, studying Bran. 'Din't plan to catch it,' he replied.

'You can come along with me. I live down here, not so far from the pub, but my folks don't like me bringing the whole mob back after lock-ins. You know, throwing up in the flowerbeds and all. My dad grows dahlias, see, and he's none too happy if they get messed up. Mel, she says it's like fertiliser, good organic produce that'll help 'em grow, but Dad, he doesn't exactly see it that way.'

Darius let the words rush over him and disappear like the cider sinking into the cloth. They were a talkative crew in Dorset. Bran snorted and clung to his barrel.

'He'll still be here come six when the pub opens again. He's always like this; he can hold his drink, can Bran, but he can't cope with the heat. Touch of sun on his head and he's pole-axed.'

Darius looked at the speaker. His skin was like bacon fat left in the sun and he couldn't have been more than sixteen. His black T-shirt hung on a rack of ribs like a rabbit's carcass and his nails were chewed down to barley seed stubs. Darius thought of himself as skinny, but next to this boy he felt solid.

'Don't know why you're bothering – he's fine,' the boy continued. It came out as 'foiyne', a word that could have had two syllables, or even three.

'People die easy,' Darius replied. 'In their sleep.' Cecil had died in his chair, asleep. But not Bran, not today anyway, he'd made sure of it.

'Come on then. I promised my dad I'd do some brashing before tea; you can give me a hand.' The scarecrow boy hopped onto the wall again and Darius followed. It wasn't as easy as it looked. The pile rocked under his weight and the higher up it he climbed the more he noticed undrunk beer slapping inside the barrels. He felt the same vertigo as earlier, impelling him forwards, and he was panting when he reached the security of the wall.

On the other side was a skeletal bus shelter, onto which the boy jumped before lowering himself to the ground like a monkey swinging down through trees. Darius followed. There was something wrong with the heat here. It wasn't as fierce as London's streets but it tired him, made his arms heavy, as though he had to push through a barrier.

They entered a small, neat garden, walked down the path into a shed where the boy rummaged until he found two axes. Darius took one, trying not to grin: a black man with an axe. People would have been barricading themselves into their houses in Tooting but this kid seemed to take carrying a weapon for granted. He led the way back down the drive and across the road towards a small woodland, Darius behind, hefting the axe and smirking.

'All roight, Tim?' An elderly man lifted his hand fractionally as he tottered past on bowed legs.

'Mr Brown, he is... used to teach me in Infants... not a bad old stick...' The youth continued his commentary as they moved into the wooded gloom. Darius was having to push things out of the way for real now, great feathery branches like warm chicken skin that released gouts of pine odour. When they stopped he stared up at blue sky spiked with green. He would never get out alone.

Tim began to swing his axe underarm, slicing up at the lowest branches of a tree. 'Like this, see? Makes 'em grow straight and thick, they do say, when you brash off the lower limbs. Forestry's got a machine for it but we can't afford one, so we does it by hand. These here are Sitka Spruce and further down we've got Blue Improved Spruce for Christmas trees, but we don't brash them, see.'

Darius swung his axe. It took off a thin branch. He smelt pine blood and watched as amber sap oozed from the cut.

Tim nodded. 'Noice one, you've got the hang of it already.'

Darius continued to lop, reversing his stroke downwards for thicker branches. Soon he was standing on a springy mat of evergreen fronds. It was addictive: the smell of pine, the gentle thwack of axe against wood, the slithering descent of each cut branch and the constant adjustment required to keep his footing. He moved deeper into the wood, cutting, stepping, wiping his forehead and feeling his hand sticky with tree juice that smelled of winter and made him feel he could inhale the world.

At seven they went back to the pub. Everything Darius touched stuck to his hands, married to his skin by sap. His hair was twisted with pine blood and frondlets, and his muscles fought against every movement of his body, wanting to slump in a plastic chair somewhere with chicken in a bucket and not have to do this foot-in-front-of-foot business. The first pint went so fast he didn't seem to swallow; his tissues just sucked the lager straight into their parched surfaces. He was drunk in a minute.

Mel was already there, lolling in the beer garden, laughing, long, pale throat stretching as she tipped her head backwards. He saw her like music: Ellington's top notes, Fitzgerald's frothy, feminine style,

Bird on a good day, giggling his horn. She filled his senses until he forgot everything else, just as he had in the wood.

'Why don't you drink in there?' Darius asked, pointing to the pub.

'Crap he is, crap beer, crap music, the whole thing.' Bran had broken free of his stupor and stood, swaying, setting up skittles in the patchy grass.

Darius went back into the pub, finding the dark tunnel from the garden just as terrifying as before, but this time the knowledge of how and where it ended made the distance bearable. The yellow light grew with every step, like a promise. Walter Trout, he thought, Walter Trout and the Radicals, *Lookin' for the Promised Land*. It made him smile: Walter looking for the righteous place and him just looking for another cold pint.

While Mike pulled the beer he checked the jukebox. Bran was right, it was crap: Celine Dion, Westlife, James Blunt. He picked up his pint and nodded to the Lee brothers before facing the tunnel again. When he made it out into the warm dusk, one hand still held in front of him to scour the darkness of holes and craziness, Mel slipped from the air like a bird and settled into his arm, lodging like a wild creature he wouldn't dare disturb. He drank left-handed all night, his right as light as breath around her waist.

At midnight they began to step over the wall again. The pub door had been locked since ten, but it didn't matter; the two-litre bottles of cider and the miniatures of rum and brandy travelled over the wall from the off licence. Only the first drink of the evening came from Mike's pumps.

She took him home. He'd been right about the wild creature. She lived in a little caravan, on a hill, cresting an encampment of half a dozen motor homes and vans. The others clustered like metallic beetles, but her wood-trimmed home stood on the skyline, looking down on the others. They glowed in the hot night, pale cubes like sugar, sweetness in the heart of them. Sweetness in Mel, anyway, as she drew him down on the narrow bed, opening her mouth to him, night-flowered with dark sugar, ripe with languor, so sex was a sleep dream, slower than a lullaby, stars hanging outside the window, eye-blinks between one moment of pleasure and the next, slower, lower, deeper, sweeter.

When he woke she was a pale landscape across his arm. He inhaled deeply, smelling burnt sugar, oranges, the gardenia from Billie Holliday's hair, dense softness of old wood burning. The morning was stealth-bombing the caravan with explosions of light, exploding dust into the air and picking out targets: the blistering metal trim of the window, a fat jar on the draining board, her frayed jeans thrown over the television screen. He had no weapon against it, only slowing his breath and holding still and hoping she wouldn't wake up. The pulse in his arm rolled slower than the others, as though her skin stilled his blood and softened his veins. She'd filled his head; her, cider, silence, the soft weight of the night heat had pushed down the craziness and made it sleep. The light was conspiring against him, tearing apart his peace and replacing it with colour and detail.

She turned. He watched the tones of her flesh change, the light stirring across her contours and making skim milk of shadows, and dune grass of her dark blonde hair. Blue veins chased her dreams across plump eyelids. Outside the flawed plastic of the window a sound rose, thrumming the length of his body like a bass note. He claimed it, let it fill him, turned it into the opening of Ray Brown's *But Beautiful* and knew it couldn't have been more appropriate. Bees funnelled into view outside, but Darius had closed his eyes again.

Hours later Mel pushed open the windows and clipped the door against the caravan side, filling a bucket with water and dirty T-shirts. Heat scoured the walls and roof, and the bass note of the long-distant bees had soared into thready improvisation, a distant balalaika chorus. Darius remained on the bed, watching the blue leach out of the sky to white heat.

He was thinking about going back to find the ugly man. The cello was calling him with its silence. He knew the man would hide it away like a miser instead of giving it to a talented young player as Cecil had asked. And anyway, he wanted to split the small, ugly mouth for its dirty words about Cecil. But there was a problem – a prablaam even. The little man might ask why Cecil hadn't passed the cello on himself, and Darius didn't have an answer.

Instead he rang the Pastor and said he'd found a temporary job in Dorset. The man's surprise was as frank as his pleasure, and Darius liked him better than he ever had before, but he put the mobile on the shelf in the caravan and let the battery die. He didn't want to know about his house, Cec-mon's house.

It was nearly a week before he saw the bees.

'Damn but they scare me, like a duppy face in the window. I jump the bed and run round the room. That Mel she laugh like I'm a poppy show, and then she say the bees no mind me, long's I don't mind them.'

He mimed that morning's awakening to Tim, who laughed appreciatively. Tim's mother handed them both sandwiches: sausages sliced sideways and laid into buttered white bread. Darius always needed two cups of tea to get the food down. Tim's mother seemed to take this as a compliment.

'Ah, Mel, she's got a way with them bees,' Tim said. 'They do say nobody could stay on the hill till she moved up there, for the bees were savage. Now the farmer can't get nobody to leave either, cos'n them bees do come and sting him whenever he sets foot nearby.'

'I thought Mel always lived there?' Darius said.

Tim's mother put thick, white mugs of thick, white tea in front of them. Her voice was breathless. 'That Mel is a bad case, Darius. I'm sorry to tell you, but she gave her parents nothing but grief. They live in the village, true enough, but she hasn't been near them for years and if you ask me, they're happy enough to have it that way. And the riffraff bunch she's got living round her... well, they're no better than gipsies.'

Tim ducked his head, waggling his eyebrows, indicating that Darius shouldn't listen. It was an awkward moment. Darius wanted to question her but he didn't know her name, and he couldn't call her Tim's mother to her face. He tried to look interested but the woman sighed and turned away.

The two of them worked in the woodland every morning and again once the pub closed in the afternoon. Darius was paid with two meals a day and at the end of the week Tim's dad handed him a twenty pound note, shaking his hand as though the money was an award rather than a wage. His nights were spent in the caravan and every morning Mel fed him yoghurt and honey. She made the yoghurt herself on the windowsill of the van, little pots in a plastic holder the colour of laundry soap. The honey came from the hives.

On Sunday they stayed in bed until noon, and then he watched from the window as she walked out into the middle of the field, stroking each crumbling beehive, insects rushing into the air ahead of her hands and compressing behind her like a comet's tail. The sound made him sick. He fought it, trying to find the song for it, shoving it up against Derrick Morgan's *Progress* and Sam Cooke's *You Send Me*, but the insect drone refused to fit, lay under the music like dirt in a grave. He twisted in the sheets and pressed his forehead to the pillow, slamming *Sunshine on Leith* by The Proclaimers into his mind, hammering the guitar chords into place against the bees, but they broke through, making mosaic black holes that entered his ears, bee by bee, and took up residence in his head. He grabbed for the biggest, worst, most ostentatious sound in the world – *Purple Rain* – and put the fat strings of the guitar, cello, violin, and viola up against the bees. For a minute it worked. Then the insistent single note broke through and levelled his defences. He pulled on his jeans and T-shirt and ran outside.

He was drunk by the time Mel made it to the pub and fitted herself into the crook of his arm. From then on he took a bottle of Bran's weird brew with him and poured it down his throat as soon as he heard the bees rising. It didn't stop the sound, but it deadened the moment when the bees crawled inside him.

His days were divided into three unequal parts. First the night with Mel, as cool as a soapstone bowl in his hand. Then the day spent in the scented wood with Tim, living a woodcutter's tale and waiting for the gingerbread house to appear between the trees. Finally the dawn, with the bees whirling, hollowing him out. He refused to let the dawn come first in the list because if he thought that way he would snap like a dead branch. It was just the bitter end of the thing, like bile after a night's drinking, or a headache after skinning up. If the bees were the price he paid for Mel, it was a fair deal.

The sweet-strong drink, sex in a narrow bed like a canoe, the long hours of sun and coolie work all made him as heat-stunned and content as a goat in a cane field. The music slipped away from him like condensation down a can of beer. He sent a postcard to the Pastor and forgot him.

The trees possessed him. He could stand in their green ocean, stupefied by the smell of winter borne up to him by the heat of summer. At first he sang to himself as he worked: reggae and old field-hand songs his mother had taught him, but the work was too heavy for song and soon he found he could only remember music when they took a break and sat against the untrimmed trees, eating crisps and drinking blood-warm lemonade. Then he could only capture tunes when he lay under the pines, drowsing through the lunchtime hour. The heat pushed the music down until he could only find it when he was flat on his back. Every night he meant to try and pull jazz from his memory before he dreamed, but Mel was always there, as cool as a drink of spring water, and he always forgot.

August made him breast-stroke through the green lanes, pushing breath in and out of his lungs, the oxygen as dense as oil, coating his innards with slow goodness. September made the leaves crisp on the trees and fruit turn rosy. He reached up one day for an apple as green as a turtle's back and knew there was a line, a rhyme, a riff about green apples, but it wouldn't come into his head. He put his hand on the tree and felt the grey bark warmer than his palm and was suddenly sick.

'Heatstroke,' said Bran. 'Get some mead down you.'

October fleshed the hedgerows with fat hips and haws, and gold light slumped over the fields where combine harvesters turned crops into money. It rained for the first time and he begged a hat from Tim's father. Mould crept up the caravan windows until Mel wiped it away.

The first time it rained too hard to work, he sat in the pub with Tim, drinking Guinness and teaching the boy dominoes. There was music on the jukebox but his lips refused to remember the lyrics Tim sang under his breath. Darius found him annoying, a mindless whinnying coming from his mouth all the time. The old men in Tooting used to say that young mouths flapped like drunken bats; now he knew what they meant.

There was something wrong about his body; his bones ached and failed to work together as though moss had crept into his joints while he slept. He remembered playing dominoes with an old white man with a tall chair so that he could get up easily. 'My bones ache, Darius,' the old man said. His name was Cecil and he was dead. He'd loved a black woman the way Darius loved Mel, given up his music for her. He must have thought he was giving up his life, but he'd lived on and on without the music until Darius came along. That was why he hadn't passed on the cello.

Tim slammed down his dominoes and Darius heard the note of complaint from the wooden table, like a low G. Cecil lost the music but lived to be old. Kept the cello alive long after his dreams had died and the woman had died. Cecil in his quiet house where the music hid in cardboard sleeves and plastic boxes until coaxed out. Cecil and music. Music and Cecil, and death.

That night the beer garden was too wet so they crammed into the bus shelter. Mel sat on his lap and they passed the bottle around.

'What's in this stuff anyway?' He wiped his lips with his hand before kissing the back of Mel's head, feeling her hair feather into his breathing.

'Honey,' said Bran. 'Mead's made from honey — thought everyone knew that, I did. Very old drink, is the mead. Very powerful. Mel gives me the honey for it.'

They walked home through wet leaves, a sound like frog bones snapping underfoot.

'How long have you been livin' up here then?' he asked her,

looking at the pale caravan lit by a fingernail moon.

She bent her head without answering and the cold light made craters of her eyes, a dark well of her mouth. Her hair frosted around her head and she barred the doorway with folded arms, leaving him hopping from foot to foot in the damp air. 'Long enough,' she said, finally.

He shivered his way inside and when she folded him into her creamy flesh he tried to warm himself, but her beauty was gelid, ice-water under him.

The next day he shivered even in the wood, pulling on his padded jacket and the stupid trilby hat. When they went to the pub he drank four rums one after another, letting the others head outside without him. It was good to sit in the bar and watch the jukebox flashing. He stood for a while running his fingers over the tracks, but he couldn't remember what they sounded like, or if he wanted to hear them. They'd told him in rehab that one day people would talk about skunk and E and he'd feel this way, like the memory wasn't quite sharp or very important. It hadn't happened. The smell of burning leaves or the sight of a powdery smiley on a little white tab could tear him open and let out the hunger like a maggot. The music had gone though, or the need for it had gone. He didn't know if he could get it back, step inside the web of sound that had held him since the day he met Cecil.

In the dark of the bus shelter, the mead tasted stale, like cheap sweets. He passed the bottle without drinking more than a sip and held Mel on his lap, knowing she should warm him but feeling her legs strike coldness through the long bones of his thighs. That night, for the first time, they didn't make love. He spooned into her for warmth that wasn't there. They slept like brother and sister. In the morning he saw fans around her eyes, creases of age and discontent. He looked away, not wanting to feel sorry for her.

The buyer came to price the Christmas trees. Tim's dad was unhappy. Tim explained as they ate their sandwiches: 'Bloody unfair! We work like stink and they take the profit. What you'd call a Babylon system.'

'I would?' Darius tried to remember. Babylon was a bad place, wasn't it? From the Bible. He saw his mother in her Sunday best, telling him he was a disgrace and that the Babylon world had got hold of him. Babylon: greasy food eaten with shaking fingers, fast tracks, hot lights, the bonfire smell of skunk, girls as packed and powerful as a grenade, and the dawn breaking over Tooting Common like an oboe playing high F. Cecil humming under his breath, the reedy sound of an old man. Any morning he saw Darius coming up the road from a gig, Cec would sing Sullivan's *Dove Polka*, like something from an old black-and-white film with the pianist thundering away in accompaniment. Babylon – in memory it was like the promised land.

'You used to,' Tim said. His mother banged down the tea. Darius jumped, coming back from the music to a cold place.

'You should be going home. Not hanging around up there with that...' She stopped, her hands at her sides, watching the window. Darius watched, too, but saw nothing. An autumn bee, fat-drunk on pollen, bustling up the pane, was all.

There was an extra ten pounds on Friday. 'Call it a bonus,' Tim's father said, but Darius knew it was the end of something, the last fine grace note of a song, although he couldn't remember what a grace note was.

They went to the pub and Darius taught Tim to drink rum and ginger wine. There was a song about wine, *Lilac Wine*, and a famous drinking tune, *Little Brown Jug*. He'd insisted they play it at Cecil's funeral. He groped for the words, the notes, heard something come out under his breath without touching his memory, a run of rich little notes like a baby gurgling. He smiled, but it was gone. He tried to find the music again. Nothing.

Mel didn't come to the pub that night. He thought about staying over at Tim's but in the end he walked up the hill. She was asleep in the dark. His mother used to be asleep when he got home from a gig, shivering with adrenaline and fatigue, and strung out until even his fingers seemed to have their own life as they rolled another joint and tapped the window frame where a pigeon-coloured sky fought to bring day to the night city.

He woke at dawn when a pale line rimmed the hills through the caravan curtains. He slipped outside to relieve himself.

The bees were awake. He watched them dancing in the dark, weaving patterns against the growing sky, remembered a whole chord sequence from a Springsteen song and a pair of sneakers tied to a guitar. And then it was lost, emptied out of him. His skull curved as empty as a melon rind, a hole where the music had been.

He walked down to Tim's house, waiting outside until the first orange light shone from a downstairs window. Tim's mother answered the door.

'Bees,' Darius said. 'They should sleep at night.'

The woman nodded.

'She been here a long time?'

She looked down and shook her head.

'She hasn't?'

'I can't tell you.'

He nodded, rolling his tongue around his teeth and feeling the grittiness of sleep there. 'But if I asked somebody, they'd tell me she always been up there, wouldn't they?'

The woman's eyes widened but she didn't nod or shake her head. Just stood, as though seeing a dead relative walking towards her. Obeah power: making spirits, taking control of things. What had Mike in the pub called Mel the first day? Witch. He nodded to the woman, knowing not to name the thing she feared.

'I worry about Tim,' she said.

He thought. The boy was too young yet, but one day Mel would turn those blue eyes on him, empty him out. Sugar Brown had stolen Cecil's talent too.

He asked the woman for money and she vanished inside the house, coming back with fifty pounds. 'Thank Tim for me,' he said. 'And thank you for your hospitality.'

She reached out her hand, delaying him, her fingertips plump and wrinkled from washing dishes even this early in the day.

'If you stop her.' She faltered. 'Well, it will be a blessing, that's all.'

She watched him out of sight, and for a strange moment he thought it wasn't Mel she was scared of, but him. Crazy thought. He'd been crazy once, but he wasn't any more.

He caught the school train to Weymouth, falling asleep. When he woke he was cold. Cold and shaking again. When it got like this, they'd told him in rehab, he was supposed to count his blessings. First: he was alive. Was that a blessing? He was supposed to think so. Second: he was clean. Was that a blessing? Yes it was. What had happened in his head with the drugs was so bad he didn't ever want it back again. The things that chased him through his nightmares were just too bad to tolerate. Better dead than that. Third... third... there was no third. Life was going to be like this from now on. Every time he woke up he'd count his blessings, get to two, and clamber out of his sleep to face a cold world. Nobody cared. If you were black and skinny you were a drug addict, black and fat you were a layabout. Black and ugly? A mugger. Black and fine-looking? A pimp. He was psychotic. That was the label they hung on him. Black, skinny, crazy Darius.

There was Cecil. Had Cecil been a blessing? Skinny old white man, head in the clouds? Yeah – he counted. He was blessed. And the jazz? That was a blessing; Cecil had possessed something stronger than drugs: a whole heap of music that could take down the fuckery in a man's head and get him righted. Fill the holes in his head that were still scummy with psychosis. Right now though, Cecil and jazz needed a little help.

Darius shoved his hands hard into his pockets and looked round the train. He found it easy to drowse in public places. The dusty seats and rattling carriages pulled him into sleepiness. He rolled himself upright and counted stations until his, connecting within twenty minutes with a spotty youth who sold him a ten-pound bag. It bulked in his pocket, singing him a sweet song. Not skunk, just a little weed, just something to fill the holes until he could get home.

He went into the Oxfam shop and bought five CDs. He didn't look at what they were, just took the first five off the rack. He sat in the bus station and listened to them one after another, slapping the silver discs on and off the portable player, mouthing lyrics that filled his head like water on parched earth. Boney M - what a laugh! *Classic Western Themes. Rite of Spring. Love Songs for Lovers.* Finally the last CD — he folded it into the machine, tipped his head back and waited. Louis Armstrong. Take it as a sign, take it as a signal, take it any way he wanted. He felt the voice infiltrate him, flushing out the bee note, adding texture to every surface of his mind.

He walked until he found a fried chicken shop. Nothing like home, but as close as he could get. His mouth filled with water as he thought of patties, rice and peas, jerk chicken. This was just something to fill his stomach until he could get real food.

The train back was almost empty. Too late for commuters, but too early for people being kicked out of pubs.

The weed was dry and pale and wouldn't roll, so Darius walked down to the off licence and bought a packet of Golden Virginia. The first joint left him nothing but the taste of burnt paper and regret. He put the bag in his pocket and went back to Mel. She was a just-something woman, like the just-something weed and the just-something food. How could he have been so blind for so long?

The moon was cold-shining through the gap in the curtains, seeing what he saw, slicing her body with white clarity, picking out a shoulder, one closed, blue-veined eyelid and a heavy sweep of golden hair. She was sleeping again.

The second joint shifted the stars in their courses, fuzzing their slow orbits until he saw their trails around the planet like a net. He heard the track: first just the spinning in his mind, gears, tape, discs and then, picking up the sounds right out of the ether, Clapton's *After Midnight.* He felt the guitar wrap him and roll him, seed of the universe.

He opened the caravan door. She didn't stir.

Clapton gave way to Bird Parker's *Dark Shadows.* He pulled his sports bag from the cupboard, judging by fingertips what to push into it and what to leave behind. As he worked he watched her face, as cool as a flower. He thought of Bran, as empty as a broken drum, Mike in the pub, refusing to let them indoors, Tim's mother, fearing her son would walk up the hill to Mel's caravan one day and come back empty of love. How many before him? A queen had to have her followers, right? But he couldn't stay, not now he knew he could still hear the music without the buzz, that endless drone, underneath. Not now he knew she was just something else to fill the holes in his head. Cecil was calling him home. How many might follow after he'd gone? Perhaps that was his business.

'I comin', old man,' he said, under his breath. 'Hold on, I comin'.' He heard Sam and Dave, the sound so clear that the aluminium window frame rattled to their vocals. And this time the song went on.

He set the joint down, the third one, and built a little pyramid of tobacco and weed, feeling flowers crumble in his fingers. He twisted Rizlas into long spills and let them trail from the heap he'd built. If the flames lifted high enough, on a chance breeze maybe, they could swing to the curtains. He inhaled, high and deep, slow and low, and set the roach in the middle of his construction. He left the universe to decide. Perhaps it wasn't his business. But he locked the door behind him, with the key he'd taken from the kitchen drawer.

They still called it the milk train, although it hadn't carried milk for longer than he'd been alive. The dawn train. The Trane's *Blue Train*. He could buy a ticket once he was on board.

He sat down on the platform and dug through his bag, finding Nina Simone. He pushed the earphones as deep as they would go, to cover up the faint buzzing that had followed him. He would get rid of it in London, where it was never really cold and the sound of life never stopped.

He thought of his house: Cecil's high-backed chairs, Bix Beiederbecke on the record player. Bix had been a man skilled at getting lost and never being found. Darius would lose the buzzing with his help. The other sounds would come back: the music, the rattle of the underground, the hot rumble of a bus on Tooting's dark streets. Maybe he would even find Sugar Brown in Cecil's house and listen to her voice rising from the scratches of a 78, freeing the stolen notes of the old man's cello through her vocals.

The train hissed into the station, sounding of steam although there was no steam. He swung aboard, keeping his head down, not looking at the spiralling black cloud that hung above one spot in the high field. Maybe smoke, maybe bees. Not his business after all.

In The
Clear

by Lucy Fry

For You of course.
Who else?

Eight twenty on Friday night and I push the restaurant door open, and there you are, tucked into a corner, dressed in tailored pin-stripe, a stiff blue shirt, your tie removed, top button undone.

You look rather handsome tonight – the first in an evening stuffed with surprises.

'Wow! You look gorgeous,' you say as I take a seat.

'Thanks.'

Gorgeous? Do I really look gorgeous? Like I'm a knockout in the sack?

'I love those earrings,' you add proudly.

'Oh. Right.'

Just the earrings, not the new dress?

I am quickly reminded why I am here: we have to talk about it. About our second kiss, two weeks ago, during that non-time between Boxing Day and New Year's Eve. It was straight after closing time, both of us plastered: a real classy street-corner snog.

The first time it happened we *did* talk about it, agreeing that it should never happen again, but clearly one or both of us reneged on the agreement.

And now we have to broach the subject once again. Because the second time at least one person starts to wonder.

'How are you then?' You start.

'Oh yeah, I'm fine.'

'Good. Me too. It's lovely to see you.'

'You too,' I agree, prompting a silence.

A few moments pass before you break. 'So.'

'So.'

'The other night?'

'Yes. I know,' I sigh, gathering my strength, because I have planned a special speech.

You are staring right at me. The sheer weight of it – your stare – makes it feel like you are putting all your sixteen stone right behind your eyes and pushing it forward.

We used to be comfortable together.

But how far can comfort stretch before it snaps?

'So,' you say again, this time adding 'Lucy' on the end.

'So what?'

'The other night, after the pub shut...'

I feel my chest judder as I let out all the air within it. 'What about it?'

'Well I thought maybe we should at least talk about what happened.'

'Really? You think we should? I mean, yes, of course we should but... Well. It was only a drunken kiss. No?'

'Twice?'

'Well no, but... Happens all the time that sort of thing,' I rattle on. 'Friends. Bored friends. Bit of booze and they're off. At least we didn't...' But you don't help me out at all, and so I spit it out: 'Gohometogether.'

'No. It's good we didn't,' you agree.

'So that's it, isn't it?'

'Yeah. If you like.'

'Well no, maybe. I don't know.' I pause. 'Can I ask you something?'

'You can try.' You smile.

'D'you ever wonder if... Forget it. This restaurant's lovely.'

You raise your eyebrows. Take a swig from your glass. If only your skin was a bit clearer, I think. If only you were a bit slimmer. And if your hands were a bit less puny. Bit more like a farmer's hands. I've always imagined all farmers' hands must be large, strong and not afraid of much, whereas your hands look like a boy's. Which is in strange contrast to your tall, hefty figure.

If only you knew more of books. Of angle and of pace. If you knew your way around a Dark Room.

Then I might be interested.

But are those things one can get over? Are those wishes that disappear?

You excuse yourself, head to the loo while I sit, as still as possible, and drink. I make a promise to myself that instead of reverting to past behaviour I shall take note of previous mishaps and tell you, as soon as you return – no, not immediately but at the very first appropriate opportunity – that both times we went beyond the bounds of friendship we were making a mistake and, although it may have been a very fun mistake and I don't regret it in *any* way (must be sure to get that bit in and not forget in midst of tension), I'm afraid I only love you as a friend.

And there it ends.

You are coming back. Just before returning to your seat, you reach down to retrieve your wayward napkin from the floor, causing your trousers to scroll down your hips and the crack in between your buttocks to become clearly visible. Not in a sexy, provocative kind of way, but more carelessly: flesh spilling over.

And it strikes me that your arse is far from cute.

I'm not sure I could ever get over that, I think. But, then again, let's not forget about belts – a decent belt and a better suit and that might never happen again.

You sit back and stretch, pushing your arms up over your head and baring a wedge of belly. I examine the way it slumps over your trouser button, lazy and uninteresting.

I know I'll *never* get over *that*, I think. But, then again, let's not forget about diets. And gyms. A healthy diet and a regular exercise regime can rectify most problems in the *belly department* – exactly the kind of comment that you would laugh at, if I were to say such a thing out loud.

You'd say the good things in life don't come without a price. Tell me that I was surely not without podge myself, and then come searching for it, with wandering hands.

Now once again we are perched across the table from one another.

The surroundings are more pleasant than expected: an up-market eatery in the capital's trendy Notting Hill. The food is Italian – the more exclusive end of the market, without a pizza or lasagne in sight. Waiters and waitresses are dressed smartly, suitably, but with a chic anonymity, none of the aprons or the napkins over their shoulders are embossed with the name of the establishment. Our waiter is very good at his job indeed. He asks politely what Sir and Madam would like to order but when Sir asks him to give us another ten minutes he tactfully makes it fifteen. Conversely, however, and more astute still, when Sir and Madam are sitting at the corner table and obviously not an established couple, with Madam betraying her slight discomfort by fiddling obsessively with the red buttons on her new dress, our waiter brings the wine faster than I have ever seen (surely something to do with the screw-top revolution as much as our waiter's grasp of the scenario), thus enabling Madam to have drunk two large glasses before even getting around to ordering the meal.

Our waiter comes back over to top us up. Then he takes out his little white notepad with a new and impressive authority.

'And what are we having this evening? To eat?' he inquires, the gap between his first and second question a smidgen too long to be quite innocent.

'I'll have just a plain green salad to start,' I say. 'And then the calves' liver with potato rosti for main, with a side order of spinach, if that's okay.'

'And for you, Sir? What will you be having to start with this evening?'

'The lobster terrine please and then the pasta with truffles,' you state without any hesitation. 'And can you bring us the wine list again? I think we'll need some red to go with the liver.'

'Certainly, Sir.'

I reach towards the bread basket and pick out the largest-but-one piece of ciabatta. I am still sober enough to know that I must soak up some of the booze but also remember that one must never appear gluttonous in company, however pissed and hungry one may feel.

'Listen,' I begin. 'There's something I really need to talk to you about.'

I go as far with my speech as originally planned — as far as the 'You're my best male friend and I'm worried we've muddied the waters a bit recently by drunken decisions and all that' — but then I lose my focus a little in thinking about your tongue, brazenly displayed as you pop an olive into your mouth. But this time we are in a restaurant so there will be no cheeky touching of tongues. You seem distracted — obviously not listening to my speech — so, gratefully, I stop, and ask what is wrong.

'Shite!' You cough. 'That's my scary godmother over there!'

'What?'

'The most formidable woman on this planet. I've no idea what my parents were thinking when they chose her to be my godmother. I used to go and stay with her. She took a slipper to my arse on many an occasion.'

'You probably deserved it.'

'Probably.'

'Go and say hi if you like.'

'What? No chance.' You hide behind the wine list. 'Only the left buttock mind.'

'What? What are you talking about?'

'When she slippered me. She only ever hit the left cheek. Scary godmother had a dislike for the right,' you add, and begin to laugh, outrageously, which turns scary godmother's head around, forcing you to sink deeper into your neck to allow the wine list to fully shield you, and now here I am, trying not to snort as one of my red buttons pops off while I take huge great lungfuls of air to replace the oxygen I have just lost (and of course now we are laughing even more, my button having landed on your side-plate, my breasts pushing through determinedly). Finally, our laughter abates, our mouths close simultaneously and instead we are just smiling, breathing through our noses and making not a single sound between us. Just smiling smiling smiling at one another in silence and it feels drastically, unintentionally intimate. Then, still smiling, just as I am hesitating over how to phrase what I say next, it happens.

You pick up the wine bottle and refill us both. 'We have a good time together, don't we?'

'Yeah. Course.'

'Well then. Stop looking so worried.'

You come forward and brush my hair with the ends of your fingers.

'What're you doing?' I smirk.

'Sorry. It's just I... Well. Does it bother you, me doing this?'

'Not especially,' I say, watchfully.

'Good. That's good.' You nod. 'I'm really happy about that.' You clear your throat. Take some water into your mouth, swallow, and begin.

The gentle giant, your schoolteachers called you.

I want a gentle giant. (A gentle giant could be exactly what I need.)

'Lucy.'

'Yes?'

'There's something I need to tell you.'

'What's that then?'

'Er... well. The thing is... the thing is that... well I... I'm sorry to do this to you but... It's difficult, but...' You grab my hand and say it fast. 'I think I'm half in love with you, is what I need to say.'

'Oh.'

Silence and, silence again.

At last, I produce words, however insufficient, however strained.

'Well that's, that's lovely. It really is. I'm shocked.'

Half in love? *Half?* Which half? Top or bottom? The man who thinks or he who acts?

'And I want to be with you,' you say fiercely. 'Tonight. I want to be with you. Tonight.'

'You do?'

'Yes, Lucy. Yes, I do. Let me explain. I...'

Even if I don't feel the same, you say, you know I care about you and, well, we were good together at kissing, weren't we? Which is always a crucial indicator that some of the *other stuff* might be all right, no, not all right, more than all right, and so... So maybe we could try and let things go a little further, what do I think?

'Right. I see,' is all I say.

But I don't see. And all I can think is that now I'm really fucked. Because now I really will have to be a total knockout in the sack. It is not that, just because you have said you love me, I will automatically jump into bed with you. Just that this complicates things rather. It is so alluring, being loved. Perhaps my feelings may be made to change, just enough to...

This kind of thing has never happened to me before and I have no idea of correct procedure. Usually when I have no idea of correct procedure I turn to other narratives for ideas. So I do exactly that right now, running through various stories in my head, thinking of what usually occurs in this type of dinner-love-declaring scenario:

I have seen films where the couple kiss and then the credits roll, leaving the viewer to suppose that the couple live happily (or unhappily) until they die.

I have read books where the couple kiss and the reader is informed on the last page that the couple will live happily (or unhappily) until they die.

I have seen one film where the couple kiss and then everybody else in the restaurant begins to cheer. (Recalling this movie, I look around. Disappointing — the other diners do not look at all the cheering type.)

I have read one book where the couple kiss and then a bomb lands on the restaurant and kills the girl.

I have read books and seen films where the couple don't kiss because one of the people does not feel the love and so the whole thing ends in tears.

But.

I have never read a book or seen a film where the person who is spreading all the love leans forward and tells his dinner companion that he thinks he may be about to die and all he wants from her is just one night. Because – pull out the trump card now, why don't you? – you believe that you have a very rare kind of cancer. Acute myeloid leukaemia is its name, or AML for short.

'You what?' I exclaim.

The other diners shuffle in their seats. I catch the waiter's anxious eye and lower my voice. 'I'm sorry, I didn't mean to shout but... Well, if this is a joke, it is seriously unfunny.'

'No joke,' you insist. 'There are still some tests to do before anyone can say for sure, but somewhere strange inside me, I feel like I already know. After all, it makes total sense, if we look at all the symptoms.'

Just to hammer home the point, you decide to list them for me:

- **ANAEMIA** – which can cause one to look pale, feel very tired and sometimes become breathless at the slightest effort.
- **REPEATED INFECTIONS** – such as sore throat, sore mouth: a result of the lack of white blood cells.
- **ACHING JOINTS AND BONES**
- **FEELING GENERALLY UNWELL AND RUN DOWN**
- **UNUSUAL BLEEDING**

'But seriously... are you sure?' I try. 'Could it not just be too much booze. And the smoking? All the smoking? It's not really surprising that...'

'Nope. I'm sure. The other day I cut myself. I was pouring blood. Pouring, I promise. It was just... unusual.'

'I see. So this next test, what is it exactly? And have you booked it?'

'Um, no, not yet. It's called a bone marrow biopsy. Sounds pretty bad.'

'A *biopsy*? Oh no, that won't be painful,' I try to reassure you.

Because I know this biopsy lark, having gone for a loop cone biopsy myself a few months ago.

'It was an invasive procedure, granted, but no lasting damage done, just the straightforward removal of some dodgy cells from inside the uterus. Not painful, except perhaps a little uncomfortable during the preliminary colposcopy examination when they insert the cold utensil. And, judging by that, I'd argue that any old biopsy is much the same. It just all *sounds* quite complicated because these medics they like to give everything a special name that other, less linguistically-orientated people will find it hard to pronounce, because it ends in -opsy or -toma, in -aemia or -itis, know what I mean?'

Your cheeks have gone a little grey.

'No, listen, biopsies are... they're... The loop cone one was, well, almost pleasant, quite relaxing. Actually. Well, that is, it probably *can* be relaxing, if you enjoy staring at the mediocre paintings the hospital's interior design team puts on the ceiling so that the patients, lying flat on their back with their legs in stirrups, don't get bored.

'But what am I talking about? Yours will be different. Much less, um... Gutteral.'

Still you say nothing although you almost look...

Amused?

Gulping down another half glass of wine in one, I feel my mouth fill with acidity, bitterness, sting. You remain convinced your time is nearly up. Your doctor said that, while it is possible the biopsy will come back clear, it is also highly likely it will not. One just can't tell. Impossible to know anything for sure.

'What about treatment though?' I frown. 'Surely if you've got this disease there are still masses of things one can do to, y'know, blitz it. Or whatever?'

You sigh. 'Maybe. Maybe not. But I think it's best to be sensible though. Prepare for the worst.'

The worst?

I do not know which way to look. Face forwards, towards the practical help I can offer? Or face back, in reminiscence of a former, carefree time? So I look sideways, and try to imagine my life without you.

It would be wholesome. Innocent. Fairly dull perhaps but certainly much better for my liver. Yet I adore you.

But is that love? Could that be translated into sex? And if it could, why have we not embarked on such a challenge already? We have been friends since our teens. There has been ample opportunity to try one another out, to take the other for a spin around the block while still young enough that nobody would think the worse of us for doing so.

'So you see why I ask?' You recommence, casually, as if you were simply ordering another pint. 'If I haven't got long, I've got to start acting on how I feel. I don't have time to sit around and... and wish.'

'No.' I gulp down some more wine. 'I suppose not.'

'So you'll? Yes?'

You trail off. Stare at me with intent.

And then your shoulders drop. 'Oh Lucy, that's great.'

'It is?'

'Course it is.' You smile.

'Right, but I...'

Hang on. Rewind:

> I haven't actually said
> I'll do it - maybe immoral,
> maybe insane (and maybe
> *crap* and embarrassing,
> although if we don't try we'll never know)
> can't let you down, what about if
> you then die and leave me alone?
> Then...
>
> there's your
> funeral there's

your coffin but
you're too
young too happy
too unfair too too
too too

Two:

But soon there might be only one.

One who now had to perform exquisitely in the sack. To ooooooooooooo and aaaaaaaaa and yes and yyyyyyyyyeees yes yes! To make you a happy man and make you grrrrrrrrrrrr and uuuuuuuuurgggggggg and pull one of those faces that men pull when they are

THERE!

(Vinegar face.)

Stop drinking, I tell myself, glugging back the third glass of wine like it is tap water, free and good for the immune system.

'Please say something,' you beg me.

Yes. Say something.

What should I say?

What do you want me to say?

Do you want me to tell you I love you?

Or maybe to reiterate your words: I'm half in love with you.

Half. In love.

With you.

I think I know exactly what you mean. Always half imagining the way that friends could be. The way that friends could love. But. If I do it? If I grant your one request? Will it keep you alive? And will you look at me differently? Of course you will; you already are. Coupled with my desperation at the thought of life without you is a vague disgust at what you have just asked me to do. I should be suspicious of starting proceedings in this way. But I am not. I just sit still, say nothing, and push all my doubts right to the furthest away parts of my mind. Best-Male-Friend-You says you may well be dead within 12 months and I am angry with you for asking me to do one thing. One fairly simple thing really. I should take some time to consider things, and really imagine what it might be like, as we are munching on our food and looking at each other in a strange, undressing kind of way. It could all be pretty straightforward really. We drink a bit more, shimmy back to your place and get into the sack. You know what you're doing (or so I am told, by the few friends of mine that you have slept with over the years). I know what I'm doing (or so I am told, by the few friends of yours that I have slept with over the years). I want to make you happy. To grant a best friend's wish. So I do. Maybe you satisfy me as well and maybe you don't. But I will have proved myself a selfless and helpful friend. May even allow myself to be called upon again for that special death-bed shag, if feeling philanthropic.

Or.

It could all get very awkward. We get into the sack and everything goes wrong. You don't like what you see. I don't like what I see. You can't sort it out down below and I can't let you in and we can never look each other in the eye again.

That's a risk I'll have to take I guess. Because I want to help you. I need to and I should. In any way I can. As long as that does not involve: watching you suffer, watching you die before you get to twenty-five, talking all the time about the fact that you are going to die before you get to twenty-five, not being allowed to talk about the fact that you are going to die before you get to twenty-five, helping you go to the loo, or reading that famous biblical passage at your funeral about how there's a time for everything, a time to die, and so it's all okay really.

'Say something,' you ask again. 'Please, Lucy, give me a bone here, I'm getting embarrassed.'

'Um.'

Throw, I assure myself. You mean for me to *throw* you a bone.

But why should I? And anyway, what does it matter now what I may or may not say? I'm going to do it, aren't I?

'How long have you felt like this about me?' I inquire.

'Since a couple of months after we first met.'

'Really? But that means we were just... Bloody hell.'

'Uh huh. You were still fourteen I think. I was fifteen.'

'Cradle snatcher.' I smile, but I am flattered, and know it shows. You shrug. 'Not any more.'

'Perve.' I smirk.

We say nothing.

'Why didn't you ever say anything before? In all those years?'

'I didn't think you were interested.'

Silence.

'Well maybe I wasn't,' I say eventually.

'And now?'

'Now...' Now I don't have a fucking clue whether I am *interested* or not, I reflect, but say: 'Now things are different, aren't they?'

'So,' you sigh.

'So what?'

'So where do we go from here?'

'Well, we can't go back to mine,' I blurt out.

Pause.

'Oh.' I look down at my plate. 'You didn't mean that, did you?'

'Not really.' You smile. 'I just meant, about us. Will it ruin things, do you think? And do you think that I'm a total shit for asking?'

Yes.

No.

I don't know actually.

Perhaps it is true, what is so often said about men and their female friends, I reflect tersely. That they gravitate towards those they secretly wish to sleep with, incapable of being friends with a woman without envisaging her naked.

And with their cock inside her mouth.

Oh no nononono, go away, no please not now too much I'll choke on the spinach as it wriggles down my throat. But I can't help it — I can't help wondering what it would be like. Yours. In mine. Lips and penis and... (Penis? Snipe nisep enips sinep spine spine spine spine spine.) Penis is an anagram of spine and anagrams never lie so it is true then, that men think with their cock. It is the backbone of their thoughts.

I know I'm going pink. Dark pink, because this is just too, too much to take in over a plate of calves' liver, however thinly sliced and perfectly cooked. I had thought truffles were a delicacy, but you are hoovering them up like Walker's Ready Salted. I do not finish all my food, suddenly excruciatingly conscious of every tiny bit of fat upon my body, thinking of love-handles, nudity and your reaction to my secret scars.

'You're embarrassed, aren't you,' you say.

'No.'

'You are.'

'I'm not.'

'Yes you are. I know you.'

Have you always been so downright prepossessing? I've never noticed it before.

'Well. Maybe just a little bit,' I admit, because I am beguiled by this 'I know you', your being unusually adamant.

'Shall we get out of here?' you ask, your cheeks softening into dimples.

'What? Now? But we haven't... we haven't finished our food. Or anything.'

'Do you want...'

'No,' I say quickly. Motion to my plate. 'I'm done with this. But you should know.'

'What? What should I know?'

Then I say clearly, plainly, with a debonair tilt of the head: 'Just that, right now, I'm completely and utterly furious with you.'

'Okay, I understand.' You nod. 'Now let's get out of here, shall we?' you suggest, wiping your mouth with your napkin and flashing your plastic at the waiter who re-emerges ghoulishly at the first sign of payment.

And then we are back at your place and already I can't remember this getting here — how long it took, how much the taxi cost. We are just standing in the hall together, and your hand is travelling downwards along my side, with eyes following, determining the details of my shape. Next thing you've already found the zip on the side of my dress and your fingers have slipped inside, as I stand, half covered, wondering what I should do next. Grease — I think of grease as you run your knuckles against me. But it is not grease, it is only water; you must have washed your hands just now when you went into the bathroom. Did you forget to dry them? Or were you too excited — nervous, too, I expect — to bother with finishing the job? What else did you do while you were in there? You had a piss; that much I know because I heard the jaunty tune of liquid playing itself against the loo. Did you look in the mirror after? Check your hair? Congratulate yourself pre-emptively on your success?

I am your trophy; I feel your nails, engraving yourself upon my skin. You exhale heavily, knowingly. Pull up my chin and kiss me.

This I know. You wrap your tongue around my own, gently, inventively, like you are trying to disarm me. But I am not yet disarmed; this we have done before. It is pleasant — more than pleasant, it is engaging. But this, tonight, is only where it starts. I keep projecting several steps ahead, to nakedness — what will you do with all my nakedness I wonder — and to the inevitable moment when I open my eyes and see that yours are already wide, wide open. That you have been spying on me.

'Shall we go upstairs?'

I nod. Why are you whispering? My hand is clasped and I am led away from the hallway where we have initiated proceedings and up the stairs to seal the deal.

The hallway is where is begins.

The bedroom is the middle.

And the ******* is where it ends. (But that comes later of course; we're not there yet.)

'My God, I love you,' you breathe inside my ear as we hover

around the bed. 'I always have, you know.'

And you don't push me down onto the covers straightaway, although I can tell from the way you kiss me that you are desperate to get on with it. Your mouth impatient, you draw back your face at irregular intervals, inhale sharply and begin again.

And I am enjoying it. I really am. But this I do not know. This is not what I have ever felt before, not with you in any case. And then I think it — which spoils it of course — I think how there was a second there, just then, a second when I was not thinking anything at all. But such glorious oblivion is quickly ruined, because now I'm thinking about how you will want me to respond to the fact that you have now successfully removed my dress, and I feel a bit ridiculous actually. And I am shivering. I am shivering because I am cold and I am also shivering because I am standing in my underwear pressed up against your suit, neck arched to reach your lips, the little hairs across my arms starting to prickle and stand up tall.

And it is *me* who pushes *you* onto the bed, not the other way around. I am up-side-down with longing and embarrassed by my lust. And it is all so...

surprising,
so very
surprising and

I must admit that I
am very
very
overwhelmed by all of-
ohhhhwwwwhmm-
this, yes... this... YES

THIS!

Until...
eventually,

making the shape of S-s-spoons with you breathing arduously yourself to sleep inside my ear I...

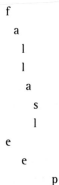

as well, although a few hours later I am awake again, trying to process information, to turn all this nonsense into sense. You look subdued. A little yellow around the eyes. You do not look at all the same as earlier. Everybody looks different when they are asleep. More vulnerable, because nobody can hide the anguish that spreads from their ears across their cheeks when a bad dream rapes and pillages its way through their precious hours of rest.

'What's wrong?' I whisper. 'What is it? Your dream.'

'It's just...' You are mumbling, lips locked by sleep. 'I'm ill. I'm ill and I'm afraid. Of dying, or not... not of dying but of... of the bit just before.'

I turn my body around so that it faces yours. Feel the sheet scuff against my buttocks and thighs and am reminded of my nakedness. And it arouses me, feeling your skin smacking against mine. So I move my face closer to you, pouting my lips and brushing them against your own, now inhaling it, inhaling you, inhaling all the fusty, imperfect man you are. You open your eyes as I continue to prompt you gently into a kind of semi-consciousness where your body is functioning even if your mind is in a fog.

There is still no light outside but our limbs are on the move again. I am arguing with myself: sometimes it is better this way. It is better when one is not alert to its extremes, because sex is like a stiffly-beaten egg white, creating soft pinnacles that stand up perfectly, seemingly pure, and yet so fragile that it can only take one nudge before they fall, turning these crests into a tasteless, disappointing mess. Which explains why I like middle-of-the-night sex best, when it is good but not outlandish, when it contents but does not thrill. When there is less at stake and there remains the pleasure of sleep to return to afterwards, rather than the severe reality of day.

'I feel... all... floaty,' you whisper in my ear, soon after it is over. 'Just like I'm floating in the clouds.' You sigh. 'Aren't you?'

I roll back over to you. 'Yes. I'm... I'm great,' I whisper, but I can't help but lie here working it out, letters moving all the time because there are enough vowels, are enough different consonants to find alternative arrangements of the contentment you have expressed.

Floating in the clouds? Anagram = staunch, diligent fool.

'Oh fuck, you're sexy,' you mutter.

It takes a while but I begin to suspect you are speaking to me.

'You don't need to say that, you know,' I reply.

'I know. I just mean it. It's true. That's all.'

But I don't believe you, and you can feel it in my touch.

'Lucy. Do you know just how sexy you are?'

'No.'

'Do you want me to tell you again?'

'No.'

Because exposing a good sentence to too much air can spoil it, force it to condense again into single words that stand alone and mean too little to be of use.

'But you do believe me? I mean it, you know.'

'Thank you,' I whisper, because you are looking at me like I am a goddess.

'You. Are. Fucking. Sexy,' you repeat, and 'Thank you so much,' is all that I can muster, because you have no idea what you have just done.

But still I cannot let it stand. Feel compelled to verify. 'Really?

You really think that about me?'

'Yes, I really think that.' You kiss me. 'And I know damn well I'm not the only one.'

There is nothing else I wish to say. Gradually the anagrams and words and questions, analyses, nerves, just soar away and yes, yes, yes I'm floating too, yes I am weightless and uncontrolled. This time I'm sure I fall asleep before you. I dream of clouds and fools who float among them but, if there is a God, I dream that he (or she) is up there, too, with all the fools whom he (or she) loves equally and without question. But this dream disappears quickly in the morning, as the Saturday rain spatters against the window of your bedroom. It continues its downpour throughout the day, giving us no reason to get up, not just yet anyway. We will just stay in bed and see what's what, see who can do what, and what that will do to whom.

~~~~~~~~~~~~~~~~~

You shake your head. 'I can't believe you're still here.'

You almost seem a little disappointed; I cannot work it out.

'Why?' I ask. 'What's so unbelievable about me lying next to you right after you've screwed me senseless for three days solid?'

You laugh. 'You're outrageous,' you say, just as a child, wishing to sound like a grown-up, might say to a pet as it scampered around the lawn. 'What I mean is, I can't believe you're still here with me, three days after we first... three days after... I mean. It wasn't part of the *deal* that you stayed. That's what I mean when I say I can't believe it.'

Yes, I knew very well this was what you meant, and yet I feel the frustration rising in me. It begins somewhere around my knees and goes right up to my oesophagus, where I let it stick.

'No. It wasn't, was it,' I reply. 'The *deal*? Yuk, that's really...'

'Oh please, Luce, you know I didn't mean it like that.'

'I know.'

But I cannot help feeling that I've been dealt. Just a little. I do not feel this when you touch me. Nor when you don't touch me. It's nothing to do with being handled in fact. I only feel a bit filthy in between my body parts, in the air between my fingers and my toes.

'Did you think I'd get up and walk away? The next morning? Or that night even?'

'I don't know really. I didn't think that far ahead. Why? Did you?'

'No. Well, maybe.' I don't know either, if I'm honest. 'I just stayed and here I am.'

'But you do... *want* to be here, don't you?' you ask.

I wriggle myself free of your stare. 'Don't be daft, of course I do!'

'It's just...' You are looking out of the window as if the street holds all the answers. 'Well, it's just I really don't want you to stay because you feel guilty. I never want your pity.'

'I know you don't,' I say quickly, although I'm not so sure.

You certainly wanted it on Friday night.

My nose tickles your cheek and now, so close, I can hardly see your face at all. Just a blur of pinkish flesh, dappled in places with reddening bumps, under the chin, a shaving rash.

'I mean, you mustn't feel obliged,' you try again.

'I don't.'

'I never want you to stay with me just because I might have leukaemia.'

'I'm not, all right? Jesus! Can you just stop with all this stoicism?'

I sit up. If I were to leave now, how would it end?

You pull me back down and begin to kiss my neck. 'Sorry. Shh! Sorry, sorry sorry, okay?'

I twist a little, feeling the chaps across your lips scrape tunelessly against my collar bone. The rest of my body prickles; it being midday, the heating has long since switched on and off again and the air inside your flat arrests me with its chill. But my neck, where you are still playing, feels warm.

As long as we keep forgetting the outside and think only about ourselves, I tell myself, everything will be all right. I have you here with me now and it is unlike anything I could ever have imagined and I refuse to let doubt creep and destroy. And yet it does; it skulks about. I feel it when the second hand of your bedside clock quivers, threatening to cheat time. But what we have, whatever *this* is, is tender and truthful, with your hands everywhere, in every moment, supervising my every move. Now you are fumbling about under the duvet, every bit the person I knew you were and also so so so much more. Should I tell you how I feel? I've never told anybody that and meant it before in my twenty-two years of life. Except family and friends of course, but that is different; they are not you. It is like we have made up our minds about each other, about your death, and about focusing on the former and ignoring the latter, all in the space of just three days and three long nights.

Your head pops out from under the duvet. Your hair, all tousled, and beneath it your cheeky, happy face.

'Lucy Fry, I love you. I love you so much it hurts.'

'Hurts? Where?' I ask impishly.

'My head. My heart. My stomach. But mostly in my bollocks.'

Laughter. Joy. We could be in an air raid shelter or on a jet ski and still see nothing but each other.

'I love you too. I really do,' I whisper.

You smile. 'Friday night was pretty fucking special, wasn't it?'

'Uh huh. And Saturday, and yesterday.'

'Yeah, and this morning.'

I smile, ruthlessly.

'And tomorrow,' you whisper.

You are risking and we both know it but I'm not about to let you down.

'Yeah, tomorrow too. And the next day.'

So it begins again: bodies, love, lust, desire, need, release... Who knows the order of importance in which they come and − let's face it − who really cares? Maybe if we stay here in your flat and never go out, just stay in bed, eating and drinking and touching and talking and giggling just like old Lennon and Ono did that time, I could forget about your illness. Maybe your illness would cease to exist; maybe I could cure you, with my love.

Well, why not? Stranger things have happened in salty waters, after all.

~~~~~~~~~~~~~~~~

Twenty hours later and we are still here, two bottles drunk, having a slurred discussion about faith. I confess to you that I have lost mine somewhere and you offer solace with the refilling of my glass. I express sadness and guilt over my reluctant belief that God is simply a conglomeration of human hopes, desires and fears, a construct of man, not disassociated with the coming of an extraordinary, yet mortal, visionary we now call Jesus.

You listen. And you nod, listen and nod. But we are not done here yet. I tell you I'm scared the white light of near-death experiences may just be chemicals in the brain and you, unceasingly stalwart, top up my wine glass another time and pull me close.

'Oh come here, you old trout,' you say, and give me a hug. 'Let's get one thing straight. You're lovely. Whatever you believe.'

'Thank you,' I sigh, and move my head up from inside your neck, pushing my lips gingerly forward, until they come naturally to rest right against yours.

And you open your mouth to let me in, kissing me better until the dawn.

Then we pass out.

Just as the sun comes in.

~~~~~~~~~~~~~~~~

When we finally awake you make a phone call and tell your boss to stick his recruitment job right up his fully-feathered anus. (You've got enough money saved for a few months, you say. You'll happily stretch it to last the both of us.) You have wanted me for all these years and there is no chance that you will waste another minute.

'What about you?' you ask.

'What? My job?'

'Yeah.'

'Well, it's hardly a career, is it? Temping.'

'Oh, come on, Lucy. We both know that's not what you're really trying to do.'

'Well, I can take a few months off, can't I?'

It might be a welcome break from the post-university void, temporary secretarial work and all my desperate efforts to get a foot in the door of a newspaper where one day I might see my name in print. People are more important than career aspirations, even journalism, I remind myself. We need to spend some time together. Consolidate this new and unexpected *thing* that is passing between us. I can work the odd shift in the pub, find some private tutoring work if I must, but you don't seem to think it will be necessary. Not as long as we don't live on Tesco's Finest and Chateau Neuf.

It is a fairy tale. A sexy, cancerous fairy tale at that. Full of malignant motives. And I am uneasy from the start because it is like you have decided that you will die. Like it is just another experience. The greatest experience, perhaps. And I am not sure where that leaves me.

But I say nothing of all this. Put it down to fear and tell myself that if I love you, you will live. Still, I agree that we shall live each day in debauched perfection and only do all the things we want.

'You sure?' you ask, excitedly.

'Of course. I'm still young, aren't I? Can get on with the career thing after. Later, I mean.'

'All right, well... if you really are sure.'

I kiss you. 'I'm sure.'

And I really *am* sure, in the instant when I say it: you are my life, my all, my love, we are together, for the moment, this moment, now, today. And no amount of words or jobs will come between us.

Until the day I wake and you are not there.

Because death will come between us. Of this you are absolutely certain. And it is catching, your conviction in your end. We can never talk about the future as other couples might. This you insist upon. No, we must never chat glibly as other couples in that first flush of nakedness and love might do, about whether we would like to move out of London when we get old and decrepit. Or whether we think it is rather cute or hideously naff to gives one's children names like Apple or Brooklyn or Lourdes. I know that your eventual absence will hurt me in my head and in my heart and in my stomach. You will not mean to, but if I had bollocks you would probably hurt me there too. Although it's too late now to stop it coming. I want only to think about us now, how real we are when we are together. Too strong sometimes. Almost unpalatable.

'You're lovely,' you sigh, content, and even having begun to believe how strong your feelings are for me I remain surprised by this unequivocal display of affection.

'My time has become like gold dust,' you declare. 'And you're the gold dust in my life.'

I hear these words, and move to kiss you, a move now so familiar that for a couple of days there has been no space between desire and thought and act. But this last comment renders my mind like a washing machine, spinning around trying to establish the fabric of *us*, to clean the wrongs and rinse the rights. But no, I am determined not to think for a few moments about whys and hows and the mess that might result thereafter, but just to lie together. Here. Now. With you on my back so that our skin touches at every possible point, your whole weight pressing down on me so that I cannot move except to twitch. It is odd though; you are a heavy guy and yet lying like this does not hurt me at all. Lying like this makes me feel safe. Like nobody will ever die. Although I can't stay safe for long; I remember I remember I remember. You must be due your biopsy soon. Any day now in fact. But we don't mention it; it is the child that hides under the bed that we can both see, and yet we know how this is played. We must not give the game away too early; we must not spoil all the fun.

~~~~~~~~~~~~~~~~

Five weeks pass and I do not check emails. Gradually I stop returning calls, and make one only occasionally to my mother, just to let her know that I'm okay. Of course she wonders where I am, why I haven't visited in so long, but I stall her with a miscellany of lies, and there is little she can do.

I lose my appetite for food, eat less, until both hip bones protrude from the sides of my stomach when I lie down. We drink wine a lot and we drink it in bed. We hardly wash the sheets, so regularly drenched are they in our love that it seems pointless to clear it up. The smell. The mustiness. I become fond of it, after a while, the little white stains and sweat marks too, but I am hardly surprised by that. Nobody ever said that love was neat and tidy and I had always thought to myself that if I ever fell in love, it would be a rather shambolic affair.

At first it is not hard to entertain ourselves. The time passes in jerky waves of body fluid exchange, and miscellaneous chatter in between, and today is nothing different. We are lying, noses pressed together, our chests still rising and falling with the exertion not long passed.

'If you were a vegetable, what would you be?' I ask.

You look at me with intent, your eyes buckling in surprise. 'A vegetable? Why would I want to be a vegetable for Christ's sake?'

Why, you say? Whereas I would say:

why not?

One tiny word's difference and yet it creeps across my spine.

'Just for the hell of it really.'

But it worries me that there is not even a twitch of recognition on your part. Don't you ever want to be something you could never be? Don't you wonder which species of tropical butterfly you would be (if somebody were to inform you that a tropical butterfly was indeed what you had to be, in a former, contiguous or future life)?

I am not sure that I want to spend my time with a man who has never wondered what it would be like to be a tropical butterfly, or a broccoli floret perhaps.

'Broccoli,' you exclaim.

Thief! How did you break into my mind?

'What about you?' You sigh. Still grateful for air, still content just to lie tightly together in the aftermath.

Await the next explosion.

'Me?'

If I were a vegetable, what would I be?

Easy!

Up my non-existent sleeve I have a here's-one-I-made-earlier answer to this question, the question that I have long hankered to be asked.

'I think I'd be beetroot,' I say, slowly, as if I have just pulled it out of the soil.

'Beetroot, urgh! I thought you hated beetroot.'

'I do.'

'Then why?'

Ah-ha! This is the more important question.

'Because it tastes kind of... I dunno. Gritty. And it... it stains your pee,' I reply, as if the answer were as obvious as your hand upon my shoulder.

'What's the colour of your piss got to do with it?'

I smile. 'Everything. You'd notice me on my way out, for example, if I was beetroot. You would remember that you'd had me, wouldn't you?'

'What about you?' I ask. 'Why d'you think you're broccoli?'

'Doesn't matter.'

'No, come on. Why?'

You shake your head, appear to be offended.

'It's not exactly like your reason. It's more... basic. I mean... I just like broccoli, that's all.'

'Oh.' I stretch my legs out. 'That's fair enough, I guess.'

You have completely missed the point of the game, and I am disappointed.

Or rather, I should say: it disappoints me that you think that you are broccoli. That you should look so pleased about it. Just another everyday ingredient. One of your five daily portions. And just because you think that it tastes nice.

'Let's play another round,' you suggest, because, I think, you can sense my frustration and you want to make things right. 'Let's do.... property or something! Would you be a... a flat or a house? An office block or a petrol garage?'

'An old schoolhouse,' I reply. 'Full of history and secret passageways. You?'

'I'd probably be a little wooden shed at the end of the garden,' you sigh. 'Not got much longer before it falls down, but still full of lots of useful tools.'

'Oh. Right.'

And again I am faced by this remembering. There is still the small matter of the biopsy. Your appointment. Pending. Awaiting us. Suddenly overriding any other concerns I have until...

'I think you're getting the hang of this game,' I say quickly, before thoughts of The Outside World can take me over. 'What about a piece of art? Would you be a Van Gogh, or a Da Vinci? A sculpture, or a portrait?'

When you utter your response it is like you are reaching out and touching me.

'I'd be a Constable.'

And I leap right on it, before you can say it. 'Flatford Mill!' I yell.

But you tut and shake your head. 'Wrong, I'm afraid. Dedham Lock and Mill. Much murkier, less easy to love. You?'

'I didn't know you were into art,' I say hungrily.

'Well, most of the time I couldn't give a monkeys, especially about the modern stuff. But my dad had a print of that one in the house while I was growing up and...'

'Hang on a sec... the modern *stuff*?' I can't hold it in.

'Yeah. Like that bed everyone got so excited about, Thingy Emin.'

'Tracey. It's Tracey. And the bed was a work of insight, vigour and truth,' I exclaim, thinking how I hate the way you make me pompous.

'Well, I'm sorry, I thought it was shit.'

'Why?'

You try to hide it but I see it: your blank look, turned helpless stare.

'Um... just that a little kid could have made a mess of their bed like that.'

'What? With empty vodka bottles and condoms and packets of pills all over it? Makes you wonder about the parents, doesn't it?' I mutter.

You try a different tack, and really I am grateful because I would never have let it go without encouragement. 'Well, what about you?' You nudge me.

'You won't believe me if I say.'

'Go on.'

'It's going to sound so stupid.'

'Come on.'

'The same as you. That's exactly what I was going to choose, and now I can't.'

'Why not?'

'Because no two people are the same painting.'

'Well maybe we can be.'

'Just for tonight,' I whisper in your ear, like I am spreading gossip.

We play the same game for at least an hour, trying to exhaust all of life's categories in the continual quest for self-expression: types of wine (you, Rioja, me, Cab-Sauv., no doubt); animals (you, not sure but maybe an iguana? And me, simple, an elephant); crimes (me, perjury, you, fraudulent dealings); reading matter (me, a train timetable, unreadable and usually useless. You?).

'I'd be an encyclopaedia, I think. Encyclopaedias have everything inside them,' you say proudly.

'But they're all and nothing at the same time. They don't really cover anything fully, if you think about it. Just gloss over masses of things.'

'Well yeah, but... Depends how you look at it I guess.'

'Yeah. Exactly.'

Doesn't everything?

Stalemate. The dawn breaks tactlessly outside. Push it away, I tell myself. Push away this unease and hide it somewhere, quick! Under this duvet, out of sight, and wait, giving you time to change my mind, redeem yourself with fingers and arms. Let sex re-marry us this early morning, enjoin what art and whimsy has put asunder.

~~~~~~~~~~~~~~~

Next it is two o' clock in the afternoon and you are making breakfast.

'All this shagging makes me seriously hungry.' You grin.

'Me too.'

'You want three rashers or two? I'm having three.'

'Two is cool, thanks baby.'

Five rashers in all, one for each week that has passed since that first night we went to bed. And I have not eaten well since, I must admit. It is your cooking. I hate your cooking. Although I love the way you stir a pan, sharply dipping your little finger in to taste the mixture. Making a kissing sound as you put that little finger to your lips (pretending it tastes good).

You fiddle with your mobile phone. Look as if you're calling somebody and then stop, as I turn around.

'Who you calling?' I ask.

'Oh nobody. Just... Oh, it's boring, just leave it.'

You reach out for me and drag me into your arms where we kiss, letting the eggs cooking on the stove behind us congregate in hard clumps.

Eventually you serve up your Eggs and Bacon Benedict, with sweet chilli instead of hollandaise and stale baguette instead of muffin, the eggs not poached but scrambled, and bacon that has shrivelled up like my grandmother's skin.

Still you manage to chomp yours down in less than one hundred and ten seconds. I know because I'm timing.

Finally I pick up my fork and eat.

'More like Eggs and Bacon Billy-Bob-Thornton than Benedict but there you go,' you observe.

'It looks disgusting, baby,' I say timidly.

'That's because it is!' You laugh. 'One of the nastiest things I've ever made for you.' You get up and grab a jacket from the hall, the blue corduroy one I like with buttons on the cuffs. 'I'm nipping out to the cornershop to buy us some goodies. Back in two minutes.'

Well at least we are agreed; I have never tasted bacon quite like it. I take a bite, swallow, and slowly put my bowl down on the sofa beside me.

'Hey wait!' I call out to your shadow around the corner of the door.

'What's that, babe?' You pop your head around.

'Miss you,' is all I say, but once the words come out I am no longer sure I will.

You are gone at least ten minutes, far longer than expected, and when you return you seem nervy, a bit disorientated, as if a small switch has taken place, enough to put us out of kilter. Like the clocks going back or forward. Or eating breakfast at two o' clock.

Is this how changes come about between two people? One goes for milk and the other sits fairly quietly on the sofa but still the alteration has taken place without their noticing? Is this all the warning that we get?

'Lucy? What's wrong?'

A stabbing pain on the edge of my left shoulder; I have felt The Outside World enter and I suddenly have a strange desire to see my mother. To hold her vein-griddled hands against my cheeks.

'Nothing's wrong. Just... You know. Paranoid or something, sorry.' Then I point to the bowl, still full of egg blancmange. 'You should tin this and market it as a diet product,' I suggest. 'I'm not at all hungry any more.'

You come right over to me. Push the bowl out of the way. Take my hands and pull me up. 'Let's go back to bed until it's dark and then we can call up for a takeaway.'

'Takeaway sounds perfect.'

Take me away.

Take me away and conceal me from The Outside World where there are rules and rationale that might just swallow us up.

'You're right,' I say. 'We should leave the eating thing till later and not waste any more time, eh?'

'Absolutely.' You pick me up and put me over your shoulder. 'My problem is I'm such a wet fart when it comes to you. I even missed you when I went to the shop just then.'

Wet Fart? Rearranges into Tart Few / Raft Wet? ReftWatArtWeftWatRef StopItStopStopI shouldstopthinkingandletyoutakemetobed.

There are no anagrams for me here. No family, no wordplay, no decent food. None of the usual obsessions.

Moments later we are right in the middle of it when you say: 'Don't leave me, Luce.'

I slow my body down and utter: 'What?'

'I know that maybe I'm not the *most* cultured guy. But I really love you.'

'I know you do. Where's all this come from?'

I brush through your hair, my fingers like a comb.

'There's nothing in the world that I want less than to lose you,' you whisper.

'Okay baby, don't get upset.'

'Nobody will ever love you like I do, you know,' you tell me. 'And you need me, you know,' you whisper, in a darker tone. 'You may not see it now, but you will.'

~~~~~~~~~~~~~~~~

We do not leave the house for another three days; I am starting to fear the daylight just as I used to fear the dark. All those others who used to inhabit my world — their faces, elbows, jowls — seem to be an uneasy, freakish memory. Everybody that I have ever known except for you has melded into a single crowd in another stadium, watching another game whose rules I no longer know nor care to know. Everywhere that I have ever recognised, with the exception of this flat, has merged with The Outside World. A world I can hardly recognise, and in which I no longer belong.

That Outside World.   Against which we stand in opposition, you and I, tenacious martyrs for the cause of Untainted Love.

Heroism? Belief? Integrity? These are the kinds of words we throw at one another. Or, to be precise, which I throw towards your frowning face, and which you seem only able to reciprocate in body rather than mind. And so I take what I am offered, grappling with it until it becomes what I think I want. But denial? Violation? Naivety? These are the kinds of words of which I should take note, yet choose instead to remain in bed with you, swapping sides occasionally to gain a fresh perspective on your bedroom, the room I now call home.

~~~~~~~~~~~~~~~~

I allow another two weeks to pass without confronting you, with doubt still hiding under the bed where I don't have to see it. We talk less, remaining close but laughing a bit less every day until one day, nearly March with the money running out, we walk out into a brisk winter's afternoon. It is three o' clock. The sun goes down in a couple of hours and we have only just made it out of bed. Our earliest rising in seven weeks. We would usually open a bottle about now and return sleepily to whatever horizontal position we might choose. But today you have a hospital appointment. I am relieved, anxious, strangely ashamed.

'I'm surprised the waiting list for appointments has been so long,' I say, chewing on the side of my lip. 'Given how important this is.'

I feel the very ends of your fingertips shirk under the accusation. We are clambering into the car. It feels strange to be outside with you, for longer than a quick trip in sunglasses and hat to the corner shop. I am frightened, suddenly. Frightened that other people might interfere. Our love has quickly become fragile; I feel protective, jealous, and a little bit like I've been skinned.

'It's not really,' you say.

'What?'

'The waiting list. It's not so long.' You look sheepish. 'I've postponed the appointment three times already.'

'You've done what?'

I sound convincing, but of course I knew. The phone calls you ignored? The handset thrown under the armchair just as I was about to take it from your grasp? (Fearful reactions, for an innocent mind.) All moments I stuffed under the bed, always hoping for a little more time, just another day, another week, before it got too overcrowded down there, no space for more denial. Because they are building up, these unsaid things, unregistered sights.

'I'm sorry I lied to you,' you say. 'It's just... I couldn't face it all. I wanted some time, or some non-time, if you like. Because I never wanted it to stop. Us. In the flat.'

You switch the radio on. I switch it off.

'And now it has?' I ask.

You look away, through the side window. Open it. Flick out the wing mirror which has been pushed in, untouched for our bedroom-weeks.

'Hey!' I try to rein you in. 'We're still in this together, aren't we?'

You take one hand off the steering wheel and grab mine. Squeeze it too hard. You are almost nodding but are clearly not convinced. There is something else going on. It could be me or it could be you or it could be The Outside World worming its way in.

'It is just the biopsy you're worried about, isn't it?' I say, knowing it is foolish as soon as I speak the words.

'No, Lucy. I'm far more worried about the weather. Course it's the fucking biopsy.'

Harsh.

You've changed, I want to say. You've really changed.

But that would be juvenile and wrong.

So? Silence, until: 'You've changed,' I murmur.

'Changed? When?'

'Just now. I didn't mean...' I start to cry. 'You're not the only one this affects, you know.'

'Oh, baby, I'm sorry,' you whisper. You are hoarse, confused. 'Of course I know you're worried. I'm bloody terrified, all right? I shouldn't have taken it out on you. I love you, yeah, remember?'

'Yeah.'

'And you love me.'

'Yeah. You know I do.'

I ache for you. Ache with you, without you too. I miss you when you leave me to go to the loo. When I nip to the bathroom to brush my teeth. I miss you when we're asleep and one of us rolls over onto the other side of your big bed. Look back on being your friend with a sort of misplaced awe. Because now The Outside World is changing everything and I think that perhaps when we get back from the hospital it may be time to wash the sheets.

We drive away from the one-bedroom flat in Clapham Common where we've been hidden for so long. The sun pushes its way through the windows in front and all around me. You turn the wipers on and douse the windscreen with some spray, and now we can see further ahead.

Now it comes back to me as you turn the car left, and right, and left. The Outside World. Where there are other ones but you.

~~~~~~~~~~~~~~~~

Soon we arrive at the hospital. The receptionist says to take a seat and someone will be right over to us in a few minutes. The walls are covered in bright pictures. As if they can make a person better, or feel better, just by colour and shapes and...

I make a promise to myself: I would give up all the colours and shapes if it meant that your AML was all a big mistake. I would change the shape of the world, if I could, or the colours of the sky and sea. Let it rain all the time, be always just ice instead of snow – just make sure you are In The Clear.

Other people are waiting too. This is The Cancer Unit. I am guessing that all these people are at various stages of a terminal illness. Perhaps some of them are in remission. Perhaps some of them are about to be miraculously cured, not by modern medicine but by faith, and by the person whom they love.

If I love you enough then I can cure you; if I believe in cures then you will live.

You are squeezing my hand. We say nothing. I think of this morning in bed and can feel myself becoming aroused at the thought of what we did, how I felt the hairs on your chest tickling against my nose, my thighs, my arms, as we made quirky shapes with our two bodies.

This is not the time to think of sex, and so I do. I can be sick in my stomach with worry and love but the mind still wanders around unguided and unauthorised.

We stand up together. But you let go of my hand. 'No, best you stay here.'

'What? You want me to...' I turn my head away, noticing that the lady next to me is wearing the same cheap, high-street bracelet as one I have back at my flat, in the jewellery box I have not opened since the night I left for supper with you in Notting Hill.

She looks a little bit like my mum, that woman. Same mousy hair, sanded with highlights. Same unbending facial features.

I swallow again. Swallow down the lump inside my throat.

'I think it's best I go alone.'

'Okay,' I manage. 'No problem. I'll stay right here.'

This means nothing. This means only that you are frightened and want to have to think only of yourself. You may even be trying to protect me. Because you love me, I know you do. And, besides, the results may still tell us what we want: that your blood is healthy and this has all been some mistake. Your bone marrow is stronger than we thought.

'Hey wait!' I yell, standing up.

You turn around. 'What?'

'Your shoelace. It's undone.'

You twitch. 'Thanks,' you say.

But you do not bend down to do it up.

'Well, I warned you,' I whisper into the air.

I watch as you disappear into a little room, where you stay for one, two, three, four... for fifteen minutes and I'm still counting. While I am waiting there are people coming in and out all the time. Some seem nervous, some with quivering lips that they are trying to keep still. Some look ill and others entirely healthy. But all of them look tired, look as if this is not the first time they've been here. A few start chatting to me or to each other.

'Hello, luvvy,' says one, holding out a plastic, coloured packet. 'Like a fruit gum?'

I am not hungry and it will get stuck inside my teeth but this man's rocky, story-telling face makes me feel this is the least that I can do.

I plant my hand inside the packet. 'Yes, thank you.'

Carefully, I pick out a dark red one. It reminds me of the blood I spilt on the sheets this morning, cutting my finger on the glass we broke last night, romping about in our castle of a bed.

'You waiting for somebody, or here for yourself?'

'Oh, no, I'm not here by myself.' I laugh loudly at the idea of it. 'I'm waiting for my boyfriend.'

Boyfriend? It sounds disloyal, saying this out loud. We have not called each other by such universal terms, not identified our roles in this young tragedy. (There has been no need, no audience, until now.)

I look glumly at my watch. 'He's been in there.' I point down the corridor. Just as I do so somebody comes out. I point to the only other corridor. 'I mean in there, sorry. He's been there nearly fifteen minutes.'

'Cancer, is it?'

'Sort of. Well... maybe, we don't know,' I sigh. 'I mean, he's getting the results of his biopsy right now, and if they're bad then he's got Acute... Acute Myel...' I give up. 'It's a type of leukaemia,' I say.

'Acute Myeloid Leukemia,' says my new friend.

'Yes, you know it?'

'You're looking at it.'

I am? But he looks terrible.

'Oh. Oh, I'm sorry.'

'No, don't be. I mean, if you're gonna have a cancer, it's probably the best one to get. Still, I think it'll be harder for you, in a way.'

'What? Why for me? I'm not sick.'

But I do not really need to ask. I know what my new friend means; he means watching you die, if it comes to that.

'People are difficult. Erratic. When they're very ill. It's hard for anyone else to follow. You can never understand how it must feel and the one with the illness can never understand why you're not jumping for joy it isn't you. It puts a... a distance between you.'

'Oh. Yeah. I guess. You're probably right.'

A distance?

It. Puts. A distance

Between you.

Like the distance in a line break of a poem? Or the distance between stanzas? Or the distance between one poem and another? How can I know? How can I tell? Does it matter whether two people rhyme? Or whether they huddle close together like words on a page?

I have learnt something today. Unlike on public transport, in hospitals it seems that people happily initiate conversations, unafraid of revealing facts about their situation, personality and current state of health. It takes the prospect of death or severe illness to make them do it, but people do communicate with strangers, I reflect, and am comforted for a moment.

Just then a tall, drably dressed woman comes through the double doors. She is heading straight towards my companion. She is hurrying, with bags of shopping. How tactless, I think, to demonstrate so blatantly the fact that life goes on.

'Come on, Jimmy,' she says as she approaches.

'It's the wife.' He pats my knee. I should feel patronised but I don't. 'I'd better go. Good luck, luvvy.'

And they are gone. I am alone again.

Good luck, luvvy.

Good luck?

How do luck and love compare? I wonder. And then I feel a squirming in my stomach; I am hungry. But the emptiness is mingled with sickness. THE WAITING ROOM. I search and fail to find an anagram for this — three words devoid of possibility.

~~~~~~~~~~~~~~~

At last you are returning. I see your feet first, walking towards me. Look up and see your face. There is a coolness in your cheeks and your eyes are glazed, betraying little.

Neither of us speaks. You take my hand. We walk out of the hospital. I can feel your tricep shaking. Wonder what this means. It must be bad news? The news that we have dreaded. The news that is bound to shatter this. Us. Our crystal cabinet of love.

You lead me on towards the car, still shaking, still silent. The streetlamps cast their glow upon the car park, shining spots of sordid orange all over the ugly grey of the tarmac. We are nowhere and in no time, as we wait for a word to pass between us.

I cannot take this any more. Tug on your arm.

'So?'

It is all I can manage.

You heave. 'I'm... I'm in the clear.'

First I breathe in. Then I smile. Then I breathe out, and hurl my arms around your neck and kiss your face, both cheeks and then your forehead, and squeal and jump about a bit, and then kiss your face all over again.

But you make no response at all.

'What's wrong?' I ask, as a nosey passer-by looks at us for just a couple of seconds longer than he should.

'Nothing,' you sigh. 'It's just... a shock, I guess.'

'It's amazing!'

'Yes. Yes, I know, of course it is.'

But you are frowning. You pull me close to you so that my nose is pressed against the nape of your neck and, although I love this getting close after a horrible half an hour of separation, I cannot help but think that you do this because you do not want to look into my eyes.

So I pull back. Demand more from you, certain that I deserve it. 'What's wrong?'

'Nothing.'

'What is it? I don't understand.'

'Nor do I,' you murmur, pressing a button on the car key. 'I think maybe we should go and get some coffee.'

I try and offer a cheeky smile. 'Or some champagne maybe?'

You sigh. 'Coffee babes, just coffee.'

I feel excitement draining out of every pore. It will be wasted on the tarmac, lost to grit and rain forever.

You hit a button on the car key holder and there is a flash of light as the automatic locking does its work.

We step heavily into the car.

At least some things can be relied upon to do what one expects, I think, pushing the power button on the radio to drown out the silence with mindless waffle. But it is the five o' clock news; no waffle here:

UP TO 13 PEOPLE ARE FEARED DEAD AND MORE THAN 70 HAVE BEEN INJURED AFTER A HIGH-SPEED RAIL COLLISION CAUSED BY A CAR WHICH HAD CAREERED OFF THE MOTORWAY. COACHES AND OTHER WRECKAGE WERE HURLED HUNDREDS OF YARDS WHEN THE NEWCASTLE TO LONDON PASSENGER TRAIN SMASHED VIRTUALLY HEAD-ON INTO A GOODS ENGINE ON THE EAST COAST MAIN LINE IN NORTH YORKSHIRE.

Another report of more conflict in Palestine. An advertisement for a documentary at nine o' clock, tracing the knock-on effects of the earthquake that devastated El Salvador.

I turn the radio off.

'There's always more conflict in Palestine. It's incredible there's anything left to bomb,' I observe.

'You got the lighter?' you ask, stretching a hand across the handbrake towards me.

'Yeah. Here it is. Wait, I'll do that.' I light your fag, which quivers around your lips as you suck on it to get it going. 'You know sometimes,' I continue, 'I think that for those who live there, the actual violence must be better than the space in between, the time spent continuing with life, anticipating death.'

'Uh huh.'

You check your rear-view, and then the sides. Indicate to go around a stationary vehicle.

'Maybe it's all the waiting, the thinking about bad things happening, rather than the action that kills us in the end.'

'Bloody hell,' you groan. 'Look at that fucker!'

'What?'

'That bloke there! He's just stopped the car and got out. Not a thought for anyone else who might have somewhere to *be*!'

'Where do we need to be that is so urgent?' I ask.

'That's not the point, Luce.'

Oh.

I am about to ask who you think you are to say what is, and is not, the *point*, but think it better I bite my lip.

So we are stuck for several minutes in traffic on Clapham High Street. Everybody is hooting their horns because a red Ford Mondeo has stopped on a double yellow line creating a bottleneck behind. It is rush hour of course. Which means that everybody is in a rush, and for a much larger portion of the day than just an hour. The traffic remains stationary. We do not speak. After a few minutes more the Ford Mondeo driver appears from a nearby newsagent brandishing three packets of cigarettes and a chocolate bar.

'Selfish bastard,' you exclaim.

'Good for you, mate,' I say under my breath.

'What's that?'

'Nothing.'

But you heard me, and I'm still thinking the same thing: Good for that man! That man in his red Ford Mondeo. Good for him for holding up the traffic. If nobody ever held up the traffic in this city, none of the drivers would ever stop and breathe. Nobody would ever just sit still and wonder about Basra instead of lurching around a corner or stop-starting the car in accordance with the lights.

Why does it matter so much anyway? A few extra minutes, when we have the rest of our lives to drink coffee together on high streets all over London, all over the country.

All over the world, perhaps?

Finally we are sitting down with cappuccinos, on brown, hard-backed chairs. You are adding three sachets of sweet'n'low to your drink.

Sweeteners? Since when did you take sweeteners? You were always so derisory about anything that imitated something else. Had to have real Coke, full-fat butter and cheese. And always pure Demerara sugar.

A woman bustles up to the man sitting at the next table. I guess they know each other but there is no greeting or any acknowledgement of the other's presence so I cannot tell how well. The man is older than the woman. He has untidy sideburns, which give the impression that they are not supposed to be there, sprayed like soot down the sides of his face. He is tidying voraciously, catching stray grains of sugar the waitress missed.

'Please,' urges his companion. 'Just leave it, will you?'

'Okay, okay, I will. Just let me get this last. There we are, see? All done.'

'For Christ's sake.'

She sounds exhausted.

She looks exhausted.

Hell, she probably is exhausted. Hence the coffee. Even though she clearly does not enjoy drinking it, wincing with every sip.

He, on the other hand, drains the remainder of his latte in one. Smacks his lips and sighs. 'Ha! Remember Jack Nicholson in that film we saw together in Brighton? Can't by any chance remember the name of it, can you?'

But she does not reply. Pulls out the *Daily Mail* from her bag and turns it over to the back page.

'Now Jack Nicholson, or whatever his name was in the film, he was so obsessed with germs that he would never sit down and eat until everything was absolutely perfect, eh? Remember that? You should thank your lucky stars I'm not like that, you know.'

I look up at you. You frown at me, a cheeky frown to stop yourself from smiling, and we are both relieved. Because laughing at someone else takes all the focus away from us. Just for a moment, but it may just be enough.

'Don't you remember the film?' The old man continues. 'The name, I mean? You always remember the names of things. I never do.'

Filling in the first clue of the crossword, she shakes her head. Her hair is blonde with obvious grey roots, and tightly cut into a bob — the kind of cut you can imagine somebody would get if they walked into the hairdressers and said, Just give me something short and neat, I can't be doing with any fuss.

'I don't want to talk about it now.'

'Later then?'

'I don't want to talk about it.'

'I see.' He pulls out his own newspaper, *The Independent*, I think, although I can't be sure because he has already folded it back upon itself so it is more manageable. 'Back to the heart of our relationship,' he sighs. 'You don't want to talk about it and I do. So.'

But this time neither of us laughs. You take a breath. Reach out to hold my hand above the table but when I give it to you, you move both of our arms under.

Under the table where nobody can see.

I have not even touched my coffee yet, although I feel as if I have drunk four already. Shaky. My skin dirtied by lack of sleep, my insides flooded with toxins.

'Well then,' you begin. 'What now, huh?'

You are laughing, half-heartedly, as if something is half funny.

But I hate half measures – so I will not throw it back – just as I hate The Outside World.

What now?

I have no idea of the answer to this question. Does anyone? As soon as you say it, as soon as one shouts the word out: NOW, almost immediately it is gone. It is no longer *now*. (Not even if a million people heard you.) And this thing we call the *present*? It is not the Right Now of things at all. It is the bit just a second or two before.

Maybe that is why changes are hard to spot until they have taken place, and then of course it is too late.

I don't remember, for example, who broke away first. Only that, just now, outside the hospital, when you and I embraced, although reluctant to admit it, I felt the change. Or rather, I suspect I noticed it many moments *after* it had occurred. That you were holding me when you used to clutch. And it was nice. It has never before been *nice*. It has been strong. Vital. Fanatical.

'Do you want anything to eat?' the man next to us says loudly to his companion.

'No, thank you, darling.'

'Didn't think you would.'

'You were right then, weren't you?'

She taps her pen against the spaces where the next clue should go. I smile in their direction, hoping that they will acknowledge me and thereby give me leave to begin a conversation. Because I'm desperate to tell someone, to say: Hey! The man I love is In The Clear, isn't that great? Yes, thank you, thank you, we are obviously incredibly relieved because now we can really start to begin our lives together, know what I mean? We no longer have to hide ourselves away, dress ourselves up in our denial.

'Lucy?'

You have let go of my hand. Left it to fall back down onto my knee.

'Yeah. Sorry. Go on.'

'You're acting a bit strangely. You seem... I dunno. Distracted.'

'Me?'

A frosty shrug, and then your sarcasm, so characteristic, so badly timed. 'I don't see any other yous around here. Nor any other Lucys either.'

'How would you know if there was another Lucy in this café right now?'

Another shrug. More frostiness. I can feel my coffee cooling, my hands wrapped around the mug.

'Can't believe you think it's me who's acting strange,' I mutter, but my words get swallowed up by the scratchy whir of a coffee grinder.

It is too much, this moment. Too laden with opportunity, expectation. It is like adding too much salt to a delicious and expensive dish: there is regret, frustration, waste. But most of all finality, no space for rectification.

Again our neighbour's voice booms out from behind his paper. 'Jesus! Says here that those with longer ring fingers have more sexual partners and more sexual desire than those with shorter ones! I've got a fairly long ring finger...'

He stretches it out in front of him.

'Why do you read those things?' she mutters. 'You always gravitate towards the crap. Whatever the publication, you always gravitate towards the crap; you've always done it, you'll never change.'

'At least in my newspaper you can tell the difference between the crap and the real news,' he scoffs. 'Jesus Christ! Look at your ring finger. It's every bit as long as mine, in fact, no, wait. It's much longer!' (He's right. It is.) 'Jesus! It's bloody huge!'

Then his tone changes quite unexpectedly and I find myself transfixed as he reaches across and grabs the woman's hand, just like you did to me a minute ago. Except he keeps it on top of the table. On top where everybody can see.

'You see,' he notes, examining both of their ring fingers. 'You and I were made for each other, my darling.'

She nods without looking up. Fills in another clue and asks, 'What's a generic term for an animal with hooves? Eight letters. Starts with a U.'

'A term for having hooves? Other than hoofed? Well. There's no such thing.' He sounds disgusted. 'Especially not starting with a U.'

'You mean you don't know.'

'Jesus!' he exclaims for the umpteenth time. 'I've got to go! I'm going to be so bloody late for this bloody thing at that bloody place. Why do you always insist on making me so late, woman, eh? My God, you'll be the end of my career.'

'All right. See you later.'

'See you later, possum.' He stands up. Kisses her forehead. Five times, I count. Five very quick kisses upon her brow before collecting his briefcase and striding off.

'Mammal with hooves,' she murmurs to herself. 'I swear there's no such thing.'

I am thinking of the various expressions on that couple's faces. Mutual frustration. Total love. Acceptance, quickly succeeded by a refusal to accept. Opposites. Repelling one another. Opposites. Attracting.

I never want to end up one of the people in that couple.

I could easily end up one of the people in that couple.

And I could do worse. I could do worse.

You and I were made for each other, darling.

You and I. On opposite sides of the table. I suddenly feel sordid and ashamed. Because we have just watched two lovers spar, held up a mirror to their lives, their natures, and still they have come out shinier than us.

'Can we go home now?' I ask, oh-so-quietly, like I am a timid, injured child.

It is almost imperceptible but I catch it just in time: your shock, anxiousness even, at my use of the word home. We are neither of us quite sure what I mean by it.

'But you haven't drunk your coffee.'

I push it across to your side of the table. 'You have it.'

But you won't. Maybe it has already started, the health kick that is bound to follow the revelation, you finding out you're In The Clear. Cut down on caffeine. No booze on weekdays. And the cigarettes? I can't imagine you without them. But who knows? Who can predict? I am beginning to suspect that anything is possible. After all... I never thought that you could look so frostily at me as you did just then.

As we are leaving I lean down towards the woman with the crossword.

'Try ungulate,' I say.

She looks up, confused.

'The generic term for hooved? Eight letters? Try ungulate.'

'Oh.' She looks down. Taps with her pen. Then writes it in. 'Thank you. Thank you very much.'

'How did you know that?' you quiz me as we walk back to the car.

'I used to want to be a vet,' I inform you. 'Read every animal book I could get my hands on.'

'A vet? But I thought you weren't that keen on animals.'

'I'm not. Any more.'

'But how can you...?' You shake your head, bewildered. Flick your eyebrows up like you hold a crummy poker hand and are trying, unsuccessfully, to bluff. 'I never knew that about you.'

'That's because I never told you.'

'Well.' You put your arm around my back. It always looks so comfortable when I see other people doing it, but I find it hard to walk with someone strapping themselves to me. 'You've told me now, I guess. That's what counts. Isn't it?'

'Course,' I agree, and wriggle free of your embrace, gingerly placing your arm back by your side, where, just for now — for the moment just passed — I feel it belongs.

~~~~~~~~~~~~~~~~

'I'm sorry, I know I'm also being weird,' you say finally, after at least five minutes of driving in silence. 'It's just quite a lot to get my head around, after thinking I was... well that I was... I don't know. I'd kind of got used to the idea and now. It's just. I don't know. I don't know where this leaves things.'

Leaves what? Quite a lot to get your head around what? Around living? Around life?

I nod. I must be strong and understanding. I must not judge this momentary lapse of sense. I put my hand on top of yours, changing gear with you, together, driving home together.

Home. (Our place? Your place? Some place where we are nobodies together and nobody can know?)

'What did the doctor actually say?' I ask.

'He said there had been a mix-up with my blood test results, that the hospital had been trying to call me for two weeks to tell me that I needn't come in for a biopsy after all and I was in the clear but... well, you know, we haven't been out much and the credit had run out on my phone so...' You trail off.

'So this was all just a big mix-up?'

You shrug. 'Guess so.'

You guess so?

'So – wait a second. You're saying all this was a false alarm? You didn't even ask the doctor to explain exactly what this mix-up was?'

'Hey, calm down. Please. No, I should've asked the doctor, I'll admit. But really I was too relieved. I think I'm a bit stunned to be honest. Maybe I'm in shock.'

'Sod shock! We could sue!' I exclaim.

'We?'

'Yeah, why not we? You've been through hell but so have I. We've been through hell. Together. And why? All because some fucking doctor probably had a hangover and couldn't tell one blood sample from another! This is professional negligence! This is obscene. I mean this is...'

'Just leave it, Lucy, please.'

Leave it? You want to just... 'What? Why?'

'Just leave it, okay? I'm going to be okay, aren't I? That's all that matters, right? Besides.' You change gear roughly, crunching it into fourth. 'It's not up to you. It's my choice, if I want to make a fuss.'

'Well... Yeah. Of course it is, baby, but...'

'Well then.' You sigh. Lean over and touch my knee with your palm. 'Look. Don't take this the wrong way but...'

'What?'

'This changes things a bit.'

'A bit? This changes everything! I can hardly breathe. All the time you were in that room all I could think about was myself. It's awful but it's true. I just kept thinking how I didn't know if I could let you go, how I would ever help you fight the disease when I was so afraid of losing you myself.' I take your head in my hands and kiss you. Deeply. Slowly. Because now we have all the time in the world. 'I don't know what I would do,' I say finally, 'if I lost you.'

The words hang around my mouth like sherbet, familiar and sharp: *The last thing in the world I want is to lose you.*

You pull away.

'Luce.'

'Yes.'

You sigh. 'Lucy Fry.'

'Yes.'

When you say my whole name like that it means you are about to say something significant, sobering. Doesn't it? Last time it was: Lucy Fry I love you so much it hurts. This time it might be:

Lucy Fry I love you and...

Lucy Fry I want you to be my wife.

Would I marry you? I have never thought myself the marrying kind (and, valuing anagrams as I do, have considered it most suggestive that marriage reconfigures easily into A Grim Era). But I just might, you know. Marry you, that is. But it would surely not be for the better reasons. Because what excites me is the furore of it all. How everybody would protest we had gone mad:

'Seven weeks of being together,' they would squeal. 'That's not long enough, not nearly long enough, to contemplate a life-time commitment!'

'Luce.' You look up, fingering my hands with yours. 'I think.... I think maybe you should go back to your place tonight.'

'Oh.'

Oh I see.

'Nonononononono,' you stammer, aware of your effect. 'Don't get like that, come on.' My head has dropped. You pull it up. 'It's just tonight. I think I just need to get my brain round all this, you know?'

'Yep.' One syllable is all that I can muster.

Of course.

Of course you do. You have just learnt that you do not have to undergo a series of unpleasant and potentially useless treatments but instead can live a normal life, whatever you may consider that to be. It is totally logical that you would want some time to sit, reflect, and to get used to the idea of being alive for several years more.

We pull up outside your place.

'Do you want to come in for a cuppa?' you ask.

'No.'

Tea will not settle this fretful rumbling in my stomach.

'Oh.' You frown. 'Well, I'll drive you home then.'

'No.'

'So you'll come in for a...'

'No, it's okay. I'll walk thanks.'

'Oh. But it's raining.'

'Yeah well. Won't kill me.' I look at you pointedly. 'Just fancy a stroll, you know.'

'All right then.'

This is not what I had supposed.

This is not how it should be. It? Us. Your being In The Clear and my walking around at night, among shadows, but otherwise alone.

I get out. Slam the door. You reach through the window, hoping for my hand.

I give it straightaway.

Tell me to come inside. Tell me you are just a bit bewildered. You didn't really want to be alone. Let me come inside and help you process all that has happened; two minds are better equipped to deal with anti-climax and adversity than one.

At least that's what I've always been taught.

'I'll call you tomorrow, babe.' You smile, gripping my hand like this is the last time.

You drive away.

I walk.

Around the shop roofs there hangs a sticky kind of light, reflecting off the cars that drive past me. I look up. Then down. Then nowhere at all. Walk on. Walk around in circles for a bit. Around the same block, past the street where my parents live, in the house where I grew up, hoping my mother will pull back the curtains and call me in for a cup of coffee or preferably something far, far stronger, which might dull this confusing headache that has come upon me since I stepped out of the car.

I cannot go in and ask for help. She will never understand. Such a short time, such a great hurt, and no real reason for this pain.

People walk past and smile, as people in this area often do, pushing buggies and clasping dog leads. They may know nothing about me, but the way I dress, the way I stand, the way I cough, tells them that I belong around here, and therefore can be treated as a friend. An anonymous friend but a friend nonetheless.

But I don't want to be their friend. I do not want to be anybody's friend; friendship seems so dreary to me now. I just want to be with you, back in your flat, incarcerated by our own untidiness. Want to be back in the bed we shared this morning, or to return to the carpet on which we made a scratchy kind of love last night. The eye mask over my face, the handkerchiefs tied around my wrists, binding me to the armchair legs — your little joke because, you said, the kind of love we shared was pure enough to allow us to make a mockery of bondage.

And of course there was this morning. We did it twice, in quick succession. First in a hurried, desperate fashion, and then more thoughtfully, you taking your time to cherish me.

I will miss that, I think, as I lean on somebody's wall and doze for a few minutes. When I wake up I am shivering. It is like I have just woken up from a beautiful dream into the middle of a freezing night alone in a tent with no way home. But I am fairly sure I have not been dreaming. I have not been doing anything in particular, except trying to ascertain what has just happened, what has just passed between us in the car, or in the time it took to walk from the waiting room to the car, or the time it took to look up from my knees and see you coming out of the doctor's room.

I want to be sick but I can't.

I itch and shake my arm but it does not go away, this feeling. Like somebody is pulling at every little hair upon my arms, just pulling pulling pulling but never pulling them clean off.

And that somebody is you.

But there is nobody here. I am alone, and I know I must go home. Home? Back to my empty flat? I have not been there for three weeks, and even then it was just a quick trip to pick up some of my favourite CDs, get some clean clothes and feed the fish. No doubt those fish (if not already dead) will be a little surprised to see me. But I walk on, in the direction of my books, my own bed sheets. Try not to think of you, try to eradicate your face, yourfaceyourvoiceyour breath (such pungent morning-breath), your shoulders and your gritty smell.

No. I must try not to do anything more complicated than
put one foot in front of the
other.

Being sure not to step on the cracks in the pavement, no, no nonono I must not step on any cracks.

I must rejoice that you are well and happy.

Must not crack.

No stepping on cracks.

No passing pavestones without thinking of stepping over all the cracks and rejoicing about this strange, long afternoon that has...

Cracked.

Our love.

No. No no.   No stepping. Side stepping. In the cracks. Don't...

But wait!

Too late!

It is too late!

~~~~~~~~~~~~~~~

I pick up the telephone, certain that it is you.

'Hello,' I say breathlessly.

'Hi, baby.'

'Hi, baby,' I say back, relieved.

'Missed you last night,' you say, clearing your throat.

You have obviously just woken up, as have I. We are still in sync then, I think; all signs point towards last night being an unpleasant blip that no longer matters. Some things are best forgotten. Left as invisible secrets that sit in silent protestation on people's walls, lost to the cracks of the pavements.

'Missed you too,' I admit.

I open the curtains. The sun shines rudely into my eyes. It is already late-morning; I have slept right through breakfast and into brunch.

I hear you light a cigarette. 'So, you coming over then?'

'Er... yeah. Guess so. Or you could come here maybe?'

Pause.

'Well... It's just... I've got stuff to sort out here, y'know. Now that I'm going to live a bit longer than I thought.'

'Oh. Yeah.' Is this meant to be humorous? I try a muted giggle, so as not to get it wrong either way. 'Of course.'

So. Those of us who never thought that we might die – apart from the obvious, ultimate, dying – have nothing whatsoever as important to do as those who had considered themselves dead and now discover they have life?

Interesting.

Half an hour later I am knocking on your door. You take a while to open it, and when you do you are topless, your boxers poking out from under your jeans. You have been wearing the same underwear for the last few days. I should know; I pulled them out of the cupboard, the last clean pair. The washing basket lies, still full, in the hallway, and pizza flyers scream: BUY-A-12-INCH-AND-GET-A-6-INCH-COMPLETELY-FREE from the floor where they've been dropped because there is no space anywhere else. Important documents and expensive items – passport, digital camera, driving licence, designer sunglasses – flung like old cracker presents across every table top and mantelpiece. A retro-style, twelve-string guitar leans against the staircase, dusty and neglected.

It is extraordinary really, given how long we've known each other, that I have never, ever heard you play.

A cigarette lolls from your lips. You place your hands on either side of me and rub them up and down my waist. Then you move them down to my stomach and start to push up my jumper, baring my chest, airing my bra.

'Hey!' I shut the door quickly.

'What? What's wrong?'

'Somebody might see us.'

'So?'

'Well. You know. Just a bit...'

'Public?' you suggest.

'Yeah.'

'Never bothered you before.'

You grin; your lips, now relieved of the cigarette, are full of suggestion.

'What? What *before*?' I ask.

And it strikes me suddenly that we do not know each other's public selves. Except as friends of course, but that is prehistoric for us now. Only the ruins remain.

But you just raise an eyebrow like you always do. Like you can't be bothered to explain.

'Hi, baby,' you mutter again, putting out the cigarette and taking me in your arms, fully this time, coming forward to breathe heavily into my ear.

Fingers running down my back. Across my coccyx. All the places

I can hardly reach myself. You hold me over the sofa. Your hands are hot. Clammy.

'We've never done it here, have we?' you whisper.

I shake my head. I cannot speak, images of you flashing like faulty light bulbs in my brain: first the frown across your brow last night and next your jaunty grin, spread now like oil across your face.

You push me down onto the cushions. You smell of stale coffee beans and you taste the way you smell. It is not a big sofa and we quickly find ourselves rolling onto the floor, where we lie together, facing one another, your nose pressed up against mine.

The sofa looks more inviting now that I am looking back up at it.

I draw back from your embrace and smile at you. Your face is too close to mine for you to see that I am smiling; have you felt my lips move? Can you feel my cheeks curl upwards? I want to show you with my smile that I am no longer upset about your strangeness last night, that we can move forward together now without any further thought of yesterday.

'Maybe we should go on holiday,' I suggest. 'You know, to celebrate your health?'

'What?'

You pull your neck away, far enough that your eyes can see me, and I think how you look a bit like a peacock, staring at me like that, chin first.

'You know, a holiday, that thing people sometimes do when they need to get away from the daily routine for a while and have a break?' I tease. 'You should really try it. Everybody's raving about it.'

I laugh. Want you to laugh with me, but you won't because, as is not unusual, I have taken things beyond the realms of joke and into irritation, and now you will not respond the way I need.

'Holiday? But you don't have a penny to your name,' is all you say.

This is not the answer I expected, nor the story that I wanted; you are not the hero I have conjured. Besides, in reality, In The Clear, you are far less enchanting.

'No.' The carpet grates the skin on the back of my hand. I want to itch it but my other hand is stuffed inside your trousers, tucked inside the button-fly of your jeans. 'But you've got enough. I could get a job when we get home and slowly pay you back.'

Maybe it is stupid but I do not even think about what I am saying. Over the last seven weeks we have shared so much that money seems the most trivial thing in the world. If I did have any, I know that I would gladly draw it all from the bank and throw it down whatever drain you wanted. I'd push it down into your trousers, just where my hand is now, if that is what you asked. If that's what turned you on.

'Um.' You pull my hand away from where it has been nestling. 'I don't think that's a great idea. I mean, I need to be a bit more sensible now. Work out exactly what I want to do in the next few months. Years even. Think properly about where I'm going. What I want to be doing in five years' time, you know.'

'Oh. Yeah. Right. Sure.'

'It's not that I don't want to go on holiday with you, baby, it's just I... I...'

'You need to invest in your future now. I understand.'

'Yeah, exactly, that's all it is.'

You begin to undo my shirt. A couple of buttons until you become impatient. Leave the rest to me.

'Sorry,' you say.

I purse my lips into a toothless smile, unsure if we're talking about my shirt or the holiday. 'What for?'

'Well, I'm not entirely sure actually. But you look sad.'

'No. I'm fine, really, just tired. So. What are you thinking of doing now?'

I skim my hands across your torso.

'Well, I'm not entirely certain what yet. There's quite a lot to consider.'

'Of course.'

What is there to consider exactly? A new job? Apart from that nothing needs to change. We are still here. We are still real. We still can't keep our hands out of each other's pants and we still know what we want next.

You start to kiss me again. Trousers come off. First yours then mine then underwear at the same time. I can't be sure until we are naked.

Again.

Familiarity draws me in, closer closer closer to you.

'Like what?' I mumble, trying to get the words out through your lips into the air.

'Like what what?'

'Like what is there to consider?'

Suddenly your hands are everywhere again. 'Baby, can we talk about this a bit later,' you plead. 'I really, really want you.'

I am so nearly taken in. But something about the way you pull a condom out of your pocket and start tearing open the packet with your teeth makes me feel a bit like a takeaway pizza that's been ordered to arrive all ready for consumption.

'No,' I mumble. 'I want to know. What are you considering?'

Are you thinking of us? Of our future? A nice, neat-and-tidy union for society to take hold of?

No.

I didn't think so somehow. Of course I've said so many times how I would hate it: if you hoped to conform like that, if you were happy with contentment. But suddenly it is me who is the hypocrite; I let these ideas scatter across my mind. And they do not look half as bad as they did in the past. Not now I'm lying here on a cold and scratchy floor, waiting to be fucked.

The room is very dark, the curtains shut with only one side lamp switched on in the corner. Looking across the floor, I can see a damp towel, obviously tossed there in a hurry, or just out of laziness more likely. Next to it are a few specks of food, toast crumbs I think; you have not hoovered in weeks. Or done any kind of cleaning for that matter. I should know because I've been here all the time. We have lain on this floor before like this more than twenty-five times but I have never noticed all this dust. How long has it been gathering, I wonder. Push my nose deep into the carpet and inhale.

'What are you doing?'

'Just waiting for an answer.'

It smells of damp wood, this carpet. Like the inside of the disused shed at the bottom of my late grandfather's garden.

'Actually I thought maybe about going travelling,' you splutter.

And I am warm again, enveloped with hope.

'Really? Where?'

'Dunno yet. Somewhere hot. Exotic. And miles away from here.'

'That's perfect! That's exactly what we need! Much better than just a holiday.' I retrieve my arms from under and over you, and throw them instead around your neck. 'Yes yes yes! Miles away. Let's go to Cuba! Or anywhere really, just as long as it's hot and miles away, just like we talked about. We could go around the world. We could... there's so much we could do. I just need to scrape some money together and then...'

'Hey hey hey shhhh, baby, wait.' You put a finger to my lips. 'Let's not get too carried away, shall we, eh?'

'What do you mean carried away?'

'I mean, it's just an idea. And, well, I'm not sure yet about... details.' You quiver nervously then shake your head.

'What? What's going on?'

Across your cheeks appear guilty lines. 'Nothing. Doesn't matter.'

'Look at me.' But you won't. 'I said look at me! Why won't you...'

'Sorry. I just...'

'Just what? Please, you're scaring me. You are really better, aren't you? It was true about the test, wasn't it?'

'Yes, it was true. It's not that. You've got it all wrong, it's just...'

'What? Tell me, please.'

You shake your head again. This time I pinch a few hairs growing from your chest.

'Please!'

'All right all right. It's just.' You stop. Draw breath. Exhale it all back onto me, right up into my nose so that I can sense more clearly than ever your muddy, brutish smell that attracts me like a car crash. 'It's just that I was thinking about going travelling alone,' you say finally.

'Oh.'

A streetlamp turns on outside. Dusk is fast approaching. I look at my watch; it says four forty-five. But even the speaking clock is not accurate enough to measure this kind of switch.

I roll over onto the other side. Look at the carpet again. Notice a small chunk of cheese. It is Swiss, full of holes. Holes that remind me of the in-betweens in things. So I push my finger into it so that it melds in with the floor and will be very hard to clean away.

'Let this cheese be a reminder to you.' I move my mouth but do not let the words actually sound. 'Let this be a reminder of how squashed you have just made me feel. How small. How full of holes.'

'Hey, baby, don't be silly,' you plead. 'Try to understand; I feel like I've just been handed my life back on a plate. There's so much I have to do. So much I want to see and I just...'

You just?

You just don't need to do any of it with me. Just don't need me any more. Now that your life has been handed back to you on a plate.

'It's fine, really it is,' I tell you. 'I understand. You just need to go off and do your own thing now.'

'This doesn't mean anything. It'll only be for a few months, you know.'

'Of course, I understand.'

'I'll get it all out of my system and then, well then I'll be back. Who knows? Maybe you could even move in after that?'

But I don't look at you. I push my nose into the piece of cheese so that I cannot smell you any more.

'It's fine, I understand. I understand, I really do...' Funny how I so often repeat the lies but never the truth. As if I want to be caught out.

'Later,' you soothe. 'We'll talk more about this later, yeah.'

Although I am not looking in your direction, I can hear just what you are doing. The puckering of plastic, your breathing becoming heavier as you ready yourself: you are putting the condom on. I do not need to look; I know these sounds and have watched you do this many times. You are quick, efficient, always making absolutely sure that everything is in place, for which I am glad now, because I want this barrier to stay between us.

Because the strongest part of me says this will be the last time. You are pushing me over, rolling me onto my back, aiming to enter from our old friend, the missionary, from which we often move like gymnasts into a plethora of curious positions. I know that you have got me exactly where you want me, and I am in your thrall, just as you were in mine that first time, after supper at the Italian in Notting Hill, your revelation and my submission.

'Oh God, Lucy, I want you so much.'

You want me. You want me and so you have me in your arms. And so of course of course of course I let you have your way; I cannot help myself because I want you too. It is a most complex equation I try (and fail) to decipher:

Hurt + Desire = Increased Desire? $\rightarrow$ H+D=5D ?

Hurt and Shock = Desire? $\rightarrow$ H+S=D   ?

Hurt x Hurt = Voracious Desire $\rightarrow$ HxH=D infinitum

It makes no sense. The more you blight our virtual perfection, the more I hanker after every drop of sweat that falls from you. To taste you once more in my mouth. The salt. The dirt. To lick your skin clean of all its irritants and harbour them instead inside myself, while you exhale whenever we draw back from one another, letting me go, piece by piece. I swallow; mostly your saliva in my mouth, I'm sure, but it has gathered around my gums and I need to get it down. Your fingertips travel up and down my back possessively; you are exploring with a kind of arrogant ownership; I am already yours and you know it. This is what we do best. But this time it is fiercer. On both our parts there is more intent. Each bead that lingers around your forehead is clearly visible now. I know how they will run from you one after the other and fall onto my own skin, towards my stomach, until they rest inside my navel. You always get a little hotter than me. Always display your passion just that little bit more; I must keep hidden the full extent of my desire. Do you see the yearning in my face? These impressions my imagination paints, of what I want us to do, of how I want you to take me, control me, love me, again again again.

I will not show them to you. Will not tell you any of these thoughts. Not like I thought you had told me all of yours.

Perhaps you didn't, after all. Perhaps I know a tiny fraction of the truth. Or a massive portion of the lie. Isn't it the same thing in the end? The facts. Pitted against the fiction. I know nothing at this point, except that there are shadows that exist between the certainty and doubtfulness.

I must allow you to offer.

I should never give my whole.

You push your torso closer to me. Just when I thought that our bodies were pressed as close as they would go, you take it further. You know what I want. You know that I don't want to ask for it.

Ask for it.

Ask for it, Lucy.

Just as I am thinking this, you slip inside, gently, politely. Like you have done this lots of times before. Which, of course, you have.

I should have asked for it, but I stayed quiet. I should have acted but I did not. If I had, there would not be this tiny part of me that feels you have broken in, like a burglar, and now something will be stolen from me that I never actually gave you permission to steal.

Go on then – steal me.

Steal me away and do it quickly, so that these thoughts might be made to stop. Oh, thank you, yes, now you are moving. We are moving together. I wonder how we look from the outside; I wonder if we look as good at this as I think we are.

And soon enough – far too soon in fact – you groan.

I think maybe I should groan back. But I don't. I can't. I can't make any sound at all. It is like you have stolen my voice too, and now you are opening your eyes, looking at me, saying hello, whispering it, hello Lucy, hello you.

'Hello you,' I say back.

Hello.

Hello you.

Why do you always say it, I wonder. Do you want affirmation that I am here? That I am really here, with you?

Well am I?

Who knows where I am these days.

Hello is just too close to goodbye to be saying it right now.

But, hang on...

you start moving faster again. This is unexpected and I love it.

And I know that you know that I love it, but I still try hard not to let you see it. Yes – I want to punish you. To make you pay for the fact that you are In The Clear. I can see what's happening here. I am being diluted. Your health has diluted me; your regained future is watering me down. Even the way you move is unfamiliar. Boastful. Like you are swaggering around inside me. Before it was different. Even yesterday, before the hospital, it was different. You moved carefully. Diligently and seriously. Like you had something in your possession that you could not bear to lose. Now you are huffing and puffing like you are running around a rugby pitch, chasing a ball, determined to score.

And I hate you. Suddenly. Preposterously. I hate your tongue inside my mouth, much more than I hate endive, the scuffing of sandals against pavement, or watching tears fall down my mother's cheeks. I hate you because I cannot help but enjoy myself. I am moving with you and we are getting close and we both know it because I am shaking and you are getting louder and yet still I am desperate that you shouldn't see. See these tears that are dampening my eyelashes. Soon you will feel them on your face but I hope that you will think they are just sweat. I want to stop, I want to stop this ridiculous sobbing, but even when I think of our happiness I can't because I know. I know that this time it is different. You are clawing at my hair instead of stroking it, pushing your thumb hard into my cheek. Then you give another moan, smaller and higher-pitched this time, then...

hold it there. After that comes the long and heavy sigh.

You catch your breath.

'Fucking hell.' You laugh. 'What was that?'

I take some oxygen into my lungs before I reply. 'You liked that, did you?'

'Liked it? That was... That was the best we've ever... I mean, that was totally subliminal!'

'Subliminal? I'm not sure that's humanly possible actually.'

I know how I am being. I want to irritate. Want to nag.

'Well,' you mumble, in a far less celebratory tone. 'I think you know exactly what I mean.'

'Subliminal?' I repeat, quieter this time, mostly for my benefit. 'No, I'm not sure I do.'

'Please, Lucy, not now. Can we just save the deconstruction for when I've...'

You are withdrawing, slowly. And this is different too; I used to feel blank, open to suggestion and exposed. Now it feels as if you haven't really gone. I refuse to acknowledge the change in temperature, the emptiness. I am holding you back because I want to have something saved up for when I walk away.

Which is exactly what I know I must do next.

I get up from the floor. Put on my pants. They are wet. You did that. Just as you have made my eyes wet now. Put on my jeans, strewn next to yours, and think how I always wished you wore more fashionable clothes, ones that fitted you better, ones that suited your bulky frame.

Put on my bra. Think how you were never able to take it off. How I always had to unclip it sooner or later, depending on how long I felt like letting you fumble about.

I love you so much that it hurts.

Think how you said that to me, only a few weeks ago.

Wished.

Was.

Had.

Already in the past and yet still I have *hurts.*

'What are you doing?'

You are still breathless. Still recovering, unable to hide your fulfilment.

'I'm getting dressed.'

'I can see that.'

'I'm going back to my place.'

You pull the condom off and check quickly that it has not torn in any way. Then you stand up and put it in the bin, where it will sit for days no doubt, still full of you. Full of your release, of your subliminal ecstasy. 'What? You don't need to do that. You've only just got here. Stick around for a bit.'

'No.'

'Please. What's going on?'

'Well... um. Okay then, I'll stay but... No. No, I can't.'

Because it is ruined. We took perfection and made it live. Now there are consequences.

Tears cover my contact lenses and, coupled with tricks of the fading light that comes in through the windows in the hall to breach the lustre we shared just minutes ago, make it hard to see my way to the door.

'Lucy, wait!'

You follow me down the corridor. I am holding the front door handle, ready to open it, stomp down the stairs and say hello to the outside.

Hello.

Hello you.

'What the hell do you think you're doing?' you ask.

'Told you.' I don't look at you. 'I'm going back to mine.'

'But why? What've I done?'

'It's nothing you've done.'

Something you haven't done perhaps. But I can't be sure what.

'Well, there must be something? One minute we're shagging, the next...'

One minute we're shagging?

'Nice,' I mutter. Then bite my lower lip.

ONE MINUTE WE'RE SHAGGING

WHAT THE HELL DO YOU THINK YOU'RE DOING?

Where does it come from, this new language you use? A language that shouts even when it is spoken at low volume.

'The next I'm going back to my place,' I say quickly. Open the door an inch. 'You'd better go and put something on,' I tell you, nodding towards your penis which is lolling to one side, in smug exhaustion. 'Don't want to give the neighbours a fright, do we?'

I laugh. I sound callous and I almost like it. I feel strong, just for a moment.

You push the door shut, keeping me in, keeping me close for when it suits.

'You're not going anywhere. We've got to talk about this. Jesus, Lucy, what's the matter? I've just found out that I haven't got fucking cancer! I've got to be allowed to think a little bit about myself! We should be celebrating but instead you're behaving like...'

'Like what?'

'Like a spoilt child.'

'Oh, I'm the spoilt child, am I?' I exclaim.

'Yes, that's exactly what you're being.'

That's your fault. You have spoilt everything. You have spoilt me.

I look up, into your eyes. 'Well if that's what you think.' I shrug. 'But you know what? When you say you love somebody it generally tends to mean you're not about to fuck off to the other side of the world without them, that's all.'

'So that's what this is about! The fact that I want to do one thing for myself. Just one selfish thing.'

'One thing?'

'Yeah.'

'Quite a big thing, don't you think?'

'What? Why?'

'Because you're leaving me.'

'What? Of course I'm not.'

'You are. You don't know it yet, but you are.' And at that moment

I can see that you believe me, and I wonder regretfully if it is too late. Have I already caused our end? But now there is no stopping me.

'Yeah, but not forever. I'll probably only go for a couple of months.'

'Whatever. You'll still be away.' It sounds adolescent and I know it. I cry.

You hold your arms out. I fall in. A few hairs on your chest go right up my nostrils.

It is at least two minutes before you start speaking again. We stay, with you holding me, me being held. Simple, but then I start to feel uncomfortable; I am finding it hard to breathe, so pull away.

'Baby, please,' you say softly, like you are coaxing a mad woman from her iniquitous den. 'Please just give me a couple of months to go away, have some time to myself, and then I'm all yours.'

I am silent.

'I promise I'll come back. We'll be together. You can even stay here, if you like. There'll be no point in renting it out.'

I shake my head.

'Luce?'

'Sorry.' I sniff. 'But I can't wait.'

'What? Why not?'

'Because this was our dream. Now it's come true and it's totally shit. It's like I'll never... oh, I dunno.'

'What? Come on.'

'I would never have even thought of going anywhere without you.'

'Yeah okay, but... but you're not the one who was ill.'

I scoff.

'I was facing death!'

'Maybe.'

'Maybe?'

'Maybe that's your saving grace then. I'll forgive you your confusion. One day.'

'Confusion? But I'm not...'

'If you really love someone then you've got to love them enough to let them go, and all that bollocks.'

'What? Nobody's letting anybody go.'

'No?'

'No!'

I shake my head again.

'Luce?'

'You don't have to actually dump someone to end it, you know,' I tell you. 'You should go on your own. Of course you should.'

But I can't wait. I won't. And I resent that you have asked me to.

'But I don't want to end anything! Please, stop this! I don't even know when I'm going yet.'

'Yes, you do.'

'What's that supposed to mean?'

I shrug. 'Whatever you want it to fucking mean.'

You hold a palm across your forehead. 'You're being so unfair. This is emotional blackmail and you know it.'

'Emotional blackmail? And you never used that to get me into bed?'

'That's not what happened.'

'Whatever.'

As usual there are words that block my view. Words that spatter around my brain like a Catherine Wheel. And questions, so many questions:

Am I allowed to grieve the man who lives?
Am I entitled to?
And do I wish to, if I am?

Where does this leave us then? It leaves us here. In a shabby, top-floor flat in a mansion block overlooking Clapham Common. Nothing has changed; we are still hanging about without clothes on. The poster of Marilyn Monroe still stares out at us from the wall, her distracted smile betraying the cacophonous despair that plays within her heart. Here we still are, yes, but now fresh details come to light.

The paint that is peeling off the living room walls, each speck just like those promises we made to one another. The tropical fish knocking its head against the side of the tank? That fish is me; I cannot tell inside from outside either. The way it moves its mouth around hoping to swallow food. That fish mimics you, your mouth moving in shock, not a single word coming into contact with the air. Yet here we still are. In a filthy flat with filthy windows that blur the filthy view of disused netball courts and the man-made pond that's been drained for winter. If I believed in its existence, I would assert that we must surely be in hell; such a swift change in temperature can only indicate a move deep underground. One minute you are ill and need me need me need my love, telling me that I am the only thing that matters, and the next you are cured, not cured really because you were never really sick, and maybe, I think, *maybe* it was actually all a big trick to get me into bed.

Besides, I'm not sure that I want you any more. Now you are normal. Now that you're so much less dramatic.

A few sentences, a night's sleep, a confused fuck and suddenly everything has changed.

ONE MINUTE WE'RE SHAGGING.

The next I'm leaving you. At least this way I am not left.

Or am I?

It only takes a certain movement of the eyes, the head. A change in sexual energy. The things you did. The things you didn't do. The way you craned your neck at Marilyn and smiled right in the middle of...

instead of looking straight at me.

No picking out some music while I am just sitting here feeling sexy. No mumbling OhGodLucy Ilovethewayyoudothat, don'teverstop, don'teverleavemedon'tyoudare. No telling me that I'm the only thing you want for dinner, or how you can taste my smell and hear my eyes. Not this time. This time it was — you were — just straightforward, determined sex. Even when we were at our most visceral, you always used to ask me how it was, if I could feel you, feel this,

that,

could I feel   that?

             that thing you did inside

just   t-h-e-r-e...

Even when we were at our most impatient, with no time for anything, not even the most basic frills (finishing quickly with only your open fly and my hitched-up skirt to show for what we had just done), you would always ask me if I was there with you. There. Here. Or somewhere else entirely? It did not matter to you as long as we did it in that place together.

It was not...

It was not serviceable, like it was just now.

'I did some research last night,' I announce.

'What? Research about what?'

'You know. On the Net, when I got home. I went on to a specialist cancer website and looked up all the facts and figures for what you thought you had.'

You shrug, nonplussed. 'And?'

'And it turns out the prognosis is usually very good. Especially if you're young, and you can handle an aggressive course of treatment.'

I linger on aggressive.

'Your point?'

'Just that if you had had AML — and that of course was always quite unlikely, given that you were basing your assumptions on a few coincidental symptoms and a dodgy blood test — well, in that case, it was still very likely that you would have gone into complete remission and gone on to live a relatively long life.'

Eyeballing you, I sniff. 'Dunno. Anyway, that's just what this website said.'

You are looking at me disdainfully; there is some suspicion there, too, revealed by the way you rub your chin, making a crackling noise as your fingers graze against the stubble.

'Well, thanks. That's... That's good to know. I guess.'

'No worries.'

I pick up my jacket and my bag, dumped on the floor by the

stairs not more than an hour ago. Just before I leave I look at you one more time, stare at the point in between your eyes to search for signs of betrayal, and ask:

'Was this all a big trick?'

We pause.

'That is the most horrible thing you've ever said to me,' you reply finally.

'Is it?' I feel cold. 'Well, maybe that is a bit harsh, I guess. Maybe you really did believe you had AML. Maybe you even convinced yourself that you really would die within a year, which is a little bit dense to be honest. I'm sure the doctors would have explained the various options available to you, had you actually been diagnosed.

'So what was it?' I clatter on, abandoning previous attempts at leaving without further words or humiliation. 'Did you really always fancy me or did you just think I was your best bet for a few weeks or months, whatever you could get maybe? Some half-decent sex?'

'Half-decent?' You scowl. 'Well, if that's how you feel. I've gotta say I'll never think of it that way.'

'Well, I will.'

That's how it seems to me now at least, in this half light. Masked by this half love.

'Didn't hear you complaining at the time,' you add.

'No.' I nod. 'You're right. I enjoyed myself every bit as much as you. Except for that last performance.'

'What's wrong with you?' You marvel.

'Subliminal.' I say the word like it's a rumour. 'I think I'd use the word rushed, if you asked me to describe it. But you didn't, so what the hell.'

Rushed.

That's it, isn't it? I have become your rush hour. I am the rush hour of your day. Although it was you, wasn't it, who said it: WHY DON'T YOU STICK AROUND A WHILE? YOU DON'T HAVE TO GO JUST YET.

How abruptly it has become moderate, our love.

A flame smoulders in your cheeks and I can see exactly what is taking place, what I am doing, all on my own, bit by bit: I am turning you inside-out. Changing your mind. I am destroying, with every word, all the time that we have wasted on each other.

You shake your head, yet again. 'I'm sorry, I really don't understand what's wrong with you.'

'I think you do. Or, at least, I hope you will, one day.'

You gaze hastily at Marilyn on the wall, then back at me. 'Is this really all just because I want to do a bit of travelling on my own?'

I shrug; the question reveals more than any answer I could give. We are already on different sides of the world.

'I think maybe you need some time to calm down or something,' you suggest.

Cheap advice, I think. But then, perhaps I have been cheap, and, yes, perhaps you've got a point. Maybe time is indeed what I require. CALM DOWN, that's what you're telling me to do. Even now my mind is filtering words, judging you on the letters you use, divorced as they may be from your intended meaning: CALM DOWN MAD CLOWN CALM DOWN.

'I never want to see you again,' I say quietly. Crucially. Murderously.

Your eyes are awash, but somehow you manage to sniff with your eyelids and keep such emasculation in. And I'm relieved; I have no desire to admit your tears.

I pull the door open and shut, passing through it very quickly to save your modesty. But you do not come after me. I walk down several flights of stairs and out the front door, colliding with an arrestingly cold wind. I look up to your bedroom window to see if you are up there dressing in order to run and catch me, but there is no sign of you. I take several steps before I realise it: I am not wearing any shoes. I have left them in the flat.

No matter.

I have seen plenty of people walking barefoot on the common, not just beggars mooching wretchedly about, but also seemingly-opulent people, classily attired in all except their footwear. One other time it was a shirt (in freezing conditions) without which I saw a man trudge listlessly towards the bus-stop. And I wondered what on earth could lead people to such shoeless or shirtless abandon. Now I think I have some idea at least: it is, it seems, not unusual to leave something of yourself behind, when you renounce someone you love.

The raindrops fall diagonally against my breast. It is damp; I'm soaked through to my underwear in less than a minute.

'People should be sensible and always be sure to split up with lovers in the summer,' I mutter dejectedly.

But I don't cry. I am finding it hard to be any more than ordinarily sad; perhaps I am numbed by the immediacy of it all. But that won't last. Even I know that. However much one is prepared for it, just like a change of season, heartbreak always comes as a surprise.

~~~~~~~~~~~~~~~~

It is the middle of March. You and I are no longer. Days pass, I do not know exactly how many, while I watch disheartening films and listen to music about hate and hurt and fear and loathing in many places not just Las Vegas.

I cannot read, having wept so much it hurts to use my eyes for anything more than seeing my way to the bathroom, where it is mostly vomit that appears. From all of me, my whole self is regurgitating you.

How much longer 'til I've got rid? Before I've rid myself of you? I am like a sheep caught in barbed wire. You have wound me up; I am impaled and making noises like a dumb animal that is unable to understand what it did wrong.

It does not get any easier. Every morning, after four or five bumpy hours of sleep, it is like I am shipwrecked once again. The desert island or some such cliché? Perhaps. I'm in the island of my bed. My purposeless bed. These senseless sheets. I just cry; I cry and I hate and hurt and fear. I remain in bed 24/7 until the sheets smell fusty, smell like I am deteriorating, parts of me passing by osmosis into this dank cotton.

This dead relationship? So much more dead than you. Who would have thought I'd be so much more dead than you? If I could make sound, I might laugh at the irony. Might choke upon the rancid taste you've left. Slimy and salty like an oyster. Once poisoned, never again safe, more easily poisoned every time.

~~~~~~~~~~~~~~~

March forces me into April and April into spring and spring brings blossom on trees, and T-shirts on chests, and Starbucks' Frappuccinos into cheerful people's hands.

These are things that used to make me glad to be alive and now cause me to don sunglasses all the time, to block out colour, diminish light.

Time passes, but it never leaves; *you* never leave. Still inhabit me, you do, somewhere within my entrails. Like a tapeworm, you've got in. And now you're gnawing at my gut.

I go over the last scene – *our* scene – a thousand times but it remains full of grey, making it impossible to judge.

I get an email from you. You tell me (and several others, not wasting your time on personal missives) that you have made some major 'Life Decisions'. You're going travelling for a while. This last year has been uncanny for you in an awful lot of ways and you think you need to get away. To clear your head and see the world.

Uncanny?

Well, that's something, I suppose. Although I can say, without hesitation, that Us, our bedroom weeks and your brush with cancer, it was all so much more to me than *uncanny*.

But still. You need to clear your head. Of course you do.

And I feel betrayal disgust surprise dismay fury regret awakening and relief because I can walk down the street without the fear of bumping into you. Then I feel sickness and despair, because I can walk down the street without the hope of bumping into you. It is a burgundy colour, this feeling. A bit like blood and a bit like wine.

And did you ever notice that bedroom is an anagram of boredom? Was that what happened, like a switch that's flicked? A few letters turned around. I became boring to you; our bedroom antics turned to boredom when you discovered you could live as long as everybody else.

I continue reading the email. There are a lot of exclamation marks stuffed in there. It makes you look a bit dense, to be honest. Bit juvenile and over-eager.

Makes you look frivolous.

Cheap.

Like you are hanging slipshod on the sale rail.

You are going away with a woman called Nancy, you tell all those lucky ones upon your list. It is rather convenient really because this female friend of yours also needs to have a break, to make some changes after working in a financial PR firm every hour God gave for the last two years. She needs to see the light of day. You are both in a similar position and so you're starting out together.

In a Similar Position? I see bodies, slapping boorishly against each other. Her legs akimbo. Your smiling face turning espresso-grimace when you are on the point of...

You and Nancy will be landing first in Mexico.

Those are places we dreamed of, you and I. Of Mexico and In The Clear.

Maybe it would be better if you were dead.

No, not better – easier. Easier for *me*.

After a couple of months in Mexico you are planning to trek/bike/drive/train through Central America into Colombia from where you will explore a plethora of South American countries. (You mention them all but I can't see because I'm crying too much and getting water all over the keyboard.)

You would like to become fluent in Spanish. Because languages are important, you've realised, and you think everyone should learn one.

Everyone should learn one, you say? Why should they do that exactly?

Communication failed us, didn't it? You never communicated the real reasons why you...

The email is nearly over. I have scrolled down completely and can see the personal signature stuff at the bottom, which says that you *will be leaving the country on April 29th after which time you will only be contactable via email.* In the last bit you say that you hope people will come and join you if and when they have some holiday and fancy going to the other side of the world. You hope that while on your travels you might learn some Salsa. Might eat the worm at the bottom of the Tequila bottle. And Nancy wants to visit Oaxaca, where she went on holiday just before her dad left when she was four, and witnessed her first and only real stabbing. She says it's the raw passion of Mexico that is drawing her there. You're more excited about Guatemala and Belize than Mexico to be honest but, hey, you have plenty of time and the world's a fascinating place so why not do it all?

Yes, why not, eh? Why not try at least to do it all?

You'd think we would have learnt by now, wouldn't you? That we never really know another person the way we think we do.

~~~~~~~~~~~~~~~

These last weeks since we left each other, I have often wished that I could be packed away in a box with all the other things that no longer work but to which people have an emotional attachment. My mother's old gramophone records, for example. The gramophone itself broke years ago but still the records sit in dusty cases behind the sofa. Very occasionally she takes them out, pulling the records suspiciously from their sleeves as if afraid of what comes next. I have never seen her actually *listen* to them; just the name of the song is all it takes for her to be back there in the midst of 1960s fever, dancing on the table with her beehive and her boy. Or driving through Provence, seven people in a mini with the sun just settling down. Making love in a couchette on the overnight train from Madrid to...

Thing is, I know all my mother's stories far too well. Surely she has no surprises up her sleeve about her youth? She's always been really into being *open* and all that jazz, too open sometimes, making me cringe and yell things like: Ah, mum, too much information; Ah, mum, please give it a rest. Although I still remember how, when I was a little girl, I was fascinated by it all and would listen transfixed. The more explicit stories only came out as she got older of course. The ones about free love and LSD, and my mother's best friend Deborah, who jumped out of a third-floor window under the impression that she could fly if only she flapped her wings.

But Deborah's body didn't die. The fall rendered her a quadriplegic. Hardly a working brain cell left.

'Lucy?'

'Yep?' I am sitting cross-legged on the bedroom floor, looking down at my body, this wasted flesh in which I hide myself.

'You listening?'

'Yes, mum.'

Listening. But only just. Lost in thoughts of long ago, times when these stories were a relief and not a chore.

'Well, what do you think?' she demands. 'Bonkers, isn't it?'

'About what? What's crazy, mum, sorry I...'

'The story! I was just explaining. We all got up at three, three in the morning it was and...'

'Sorry, of course. Funny, I mean uh... yeah...'

Three o'clock? A three o'clock in the morning story? The one about the night in the Andalusian police cell or the one about the Sandy Shaw gig, the after-party or whatever?

'You haven't been listening to a word I've said. Honestly. Are you all right?'

'Sorry, mum.'

'Sometimes I wonder why you call.'

'Well, I...'

I didn't. In fact I haven't called my mother in a fortnight. It was she who called me, just like the last time. Beginning with a gripe about the packers in Waitrose who put the twelve-pack of eggs on the bottom and all the tins of tomatoes on the top.

She wouldn't have minded so much if it was just a six-pack, mum has already explained. But a twelve-pack! Eggs are not so cheap these days. Especially if, like one should (and like she does), one buys *free range.*

'Are you all right, darling?' she asks again.

'Sorry, yeah. I'm okay, I guess.'

'You guess?'

'Yeah.'

'Your father and I will always support you, you know. Whatever it is you need to tell us.'

'I don't have anything to tell you. Honestly.'

She sighs, and then: 'Because it would be nice...' She pauses. '... if we started to do things, as a family again.'

To do things 'as a family'. A long-term favourite phrase of hers.

The phone crackles, and then silence until:

'Yeah, I know. I'm sorry, mum. We'll do something together soon. Or if not right now then there's always Christmas to look forward to,' I add, because I know it will really get her going.

'But it's only May! Christmas is months away!'

'Sorry. Just a joke.'

'I see.'

I find the strangest things funny these days. The homeless person that I saw lying on the street corner the other day – I actually had to stifle a laugh when I noticed the way his bull terrier was nibbling at his trainer. And then, not long after, I was watching *The Hours* again (fifth time this month) and found myself cackling at the bit when the Joycean figure, Richard, slides off the window ledge and falls to his death below.

Yes, I'm afraid it is true. I have been laughing at these things.

They are all mixed up, the laughter and the tears.

'How about Sunday then?' she suggests. 'I'll cook us a shoulder of lamb.'

'Can't do Sunday, mum, sorry.'

'Why? Why not? What are you doing that's so important?'

'Oh, you know. Just stuff.'

Got an appointment.

A very important appointment under the covers. With my id, my ego and my superego. We are all going to have a party, just us, and maybe with a bit of snot and tears.

'I thought you loved shoulder of lamb?'

'I do. Speak to you soon.'

'Okay then, if you've got to go...'

'Bye, mum.'

'Oh wait, Lucy -'

But I have put the phone down before she can finish. I get up to press Play on the ageing hi-fi in the corner of my room, whose coffee-stained speakers force out the music with diminishing enthusiasm each time I use them. I listen for the quick sizzle so I know the disc is spinning and I can curl up in the corner and wait.

It is starting. These lyrics – first they pinch at my skin, but that is before the biting starts. A man sings to his lover of striking chords, of memories and regret.

Chunks are taken out of me, my heart is chewed.

I am half singing, half keeping quiet. Holding myself back so that I won't remember why it is I am trying not to remember. You. Me. That last time.

Turning the volume dial, I wait until the speakers shudder under the pressure of these thick, scratchy harmonies.

I have lost track of the parts of myself I liked the most, and knew the best. But still I can't remember. Shouldn't. Mustn't.

That night on the common – when I was shoeless, feeling the twigs scratching at my heels – I made a decision. I told myself that, from then on, I would keep myself locked up like a schoolgirl's tuck box, forever suspicious that if you share a little bit then people always ask for more. I told myself that I was sick of sharing; I'd rather have all the best bits to myself, because otherwise people would just take what they liked from me and then leave the rest.

The phone is ringing again. It is within arm's reach but I make no move to answer it, sit still for a while and wait, having decided that tonight I will devote myself completely and utterly to drunkenness and the most depressing songs that I possess in my collection.

But the phone is still ringing.

It has rung thirty-five times now.

And make that thirty-six. Thirty-se...

I grab the handset. If I don't get it, she will only come round instead.

'Mum?'

'I knew you were there. I just knew.'

'Of course I'm here. I'm always here.'

'So. How are you?'

'Fine. Same as half an hour ago, last time we spoke.'

'Darling, you sound tired. Were you out very late last night?'

'No.'

Oh, what a lie! What a fat, pulsing, gratuitous lie.

'Sure?'

'Depends what you call *out*, I guess.'

This is fairer.

'Few drinks with an old friend,' I reveal.

'Oh. Nice.'

No. Not nice. Grubby. Deliberate. Six vodkas in the pub. Another couple at his place, all of which culminated in a quick blow job on the floor behind the old friend's sofa.

There is nothing left in me but instinct.

'Yes,' I say. 'It was quite nice to see him, I guess.'

'Look, Lucy, I just called because... Well, because I... Well, I just wanted to hear your voice.'

'Well. Here I am.'

'I know, yes, there you are. But you sound so...'

What? What do I sound?

I decide to help her out. 'Distant?'

'Yes. Yes, distant. And you seem ever so down.'

'I'm sorry, mum.'

I feel a little nauseous – Argentinean Shiraz, I've drunk nearly the entire bottle.

'I love you very much, my darling. Always have, always will. Whatever you have done, and whatever you might do.'

She always says this, as if I am a criminal, leaning heavily on the words 'very' and 'much'. I would give her one of my disdainful huffs if I could be bothered. I still respond in thought, which I suppose is a good sign: Dear mum, I only wish you were right, that love was quantifiable as you make out, as you truly believe it is.

'I'm always here for you, you know that.' There is pain in her voice. 'If you change your mind about Sunday, I'll be cooking your favourite anyway. Just so you know.'

'Thanks. But I really can't. Not this time. Not this week.'

'All right, darling. Sleep well then.'

'Thanks, yeah, I will,' I reply, and she hangs up.

But I will not be sleeping much tonight. I think we're both aware of that. And when I do finally fall into boozy unconsciousness, I have a dream of you. It is that anomaly, a Real Dream, in the sense that my dream fits the facts absolutely, of our driving back that afternoon, after the hospital, fresh with the knowledge that you were In The Clear, the day before our last time.

And I wake up crying – the sun still sleeping – shivering, alone.

~~~~~~~~~~~~~~~~~

Spring moves into summer, with a blurry week somewhere between. In the evenings either I lie in bed and watch TV or else I drink myself into an amoebic stupor. It's four months since I left your flat for the last time. I have a job. My days are spent working in a café on a quaint South London street where well-to-do young mothers bring their buggies so that their kids can all scream together about how much they hate it when their mum spits on a napkin to wipe the croissant from round their mouth. On an average day I spill things, make mistakes with bills, do not come close to breaking into a smile, and I never, ever get any tips. It is only four pounds an hour. Nobody but crazy students, or former wordsmiths who are now so anaesthetized they cannot sense, let alone express, what they are feeling, would work for such a shitty wage. The hours are eight till six on a good day. I am on my feet all the time, with thirty minutes for lunch – too long: I do not know where to go, don't want to eat, and have made no friends among the other staff, so wander aimlessly up and down the road, sporting an egg-splashed, fat-sprinkled apron that makes me smell like I've doused myself in oil and rubbed bacon rind across my neck. All the customers mutter about how crap I am at my job but they never say a nasty word to me in person. I suspect I wear a look that says Don't fuck me off or I just won't bring you your food. These mothers are so desperate to feed their truculent kids that they don't have the energy to complain about the shoddy service they receive from me. The manager is so desperate for staff that she does not sack me, just pays me a pittance for doing a poor job in a wealthy area. And me? I am just so generally, utterly, pointlessly desperate that I don't tell them to shove their bullshit job right up their anus because I got a solid degree from a respected University and could be doing a myriad of other things right now.

What could I do exactly?

What have I done, except lose you?

You have left me with nothing. What can I do with nothing? I can't even throw it away. It just hangs around, like something, nothing does.

My mother pops by the café daily at eleven. Comes for a coffee and a chat, she says. But really she does it just to check that I am still working. That I've not melted underneath the duvet. Days get longer; the daylight makes it harder; in darkness I can try and pretend that I'm not here.

People try to keep in touch. But these days conversations with me tend to go something like this:

'Hey, Lucy. How are you?'

'Fine.' (Fucked-up, Insecure, Neurotic and Emotional)

'Good. How's the waitressing job?'

'Fine.'

'And how's other stuff?'

'Yep, that's fine. Other stuff is fine.'

'Any gossip?'

'No.'

'Boyfriend?'

'No.'

'Anything good going on?'

'No.'

'Something wrong?'

'No.'

'Sure?'

'No.'

'Want to talk about it?'

'No.'

'Maybe I should leave you to it then.'

'If you like.'

'Oh, okay then. Well, I'd better get on. I'll call you again in a week or so. See how you're getting on.'

'If you like.'

'All right then. Bye.'

Only my mother keeps on calling. Visiting. Nipping in for a quick coffee. That's the thing about good mothers, however disastrously neurotic they might be: they never leave you alone to really, *really* fall apart. Which is why, inevitably, conversations with her contain a little more substance than with the others.

There is one conversation in particular that changes things. It prickles my skin and I can feel her crawling in. I push her away away away but still she crawls and crawls, as if on hands and knees, until I have no choice.

It is July, a pleasant temperature, the end of my shift when she comes by:

'Hello, darling.'

'Hi, mum. How are you?'

'Well, I'm okay, I suppose.' She takes a breath. 'Except I'm awfully worried about you.'

Shrug. 'Don't be. I'm fine.'

'Please don't insult me, Lucy,' she bustles. 'I'm still your mother, whatever you may feel towards me.'

Feel towards her? I don't feel anything towards her. Nothing bad at least. Why must everybody take my withdrawl so personally?

'Darling, please talk to me. This has gone on for long enough. I demand to know.'

Demand?

'You can demand all you like,' I mutter.

'What's that?'

'I said I don't know what to tell you.'

'The truth might be a start.'

'There is no truth. Unless you can show me where he keeps it hidden. Your God, I mean.'

'Oh please don't start that again, Lucy. What's happened? Where've you gone?' She touches my side, feels the bones protruding through my shirt. 'You're not eating, are you? You can't have been eating anything.'

'Course I have. I'd be dead by now, if I hadn't.'

'What is it? You can tell me. You can tell me anything you want, you know that.'

Anything I want?

Can I tell her to fuck off?

'Please, mum. Just... Just leave me alone. I'll be fine in a few weeks. I just need a bit of space.'

She shakes her head. Bites her lip. 'Darling, it's a lonely road you're choosing. I'm not sure you fully realise just how lonely.'

Oh, no, don't you bloody start as well. Please. No, no, don't you...

Oh God, she's blubbing.

'Shhh, mum, please, listen.' I rub her shoulder. Her back. The first person I have touched with any warmth since...

'Mum, look, it's nothing, okay? I'm sorry. It's not your fault. It's nothing to do with you.'

'Of course it's to do with me,' she wails. 'You're my baby.... my baby... my... OhJesusLucy, you'renotareyou? You're not pregnant, are you?'

'No. No, mum, I'm not pregnant.'

'Oh, thank God.' She stops crying. Thinks. 'So... is it...' She is trembling. 'Are you taking something? Do you have a problem with... Do you have a drug problem, my darling? You can tell me. Don't be ashamed.'

'No, mum. No drugs.'

Although that might be better. To crave a substance instead of you.

'Is it a boy?'

I snap my head up and glare, but she will not correct herself. She knows how it irritates me. Only her little girl can love a boy, while her young woman sleeps with men.

I shake my head. 'No. No man involved.'

'You're lying, darling. I can tell. I've always been able to tell.'

Shake my head again.

Fuck.

No.

Don't ask me that.

'Lucy. What happened? Tell your old mum what's been going on, eh?'

No.

No telling. No letting secrets go no telling about *you* no letting go of my secret you no letting *go*.

I heave.

I lurch from foot to foot. Hit my head against a nearby wall until she starts crying again, which is the only thing that makes me stop.

It is a simple equation really: if I begin to let her in, then I begin to let you go.

'Lucy, no, don't do that don't hurt yourself like that come on come here shhh baby just come here it's okay just talk just talk just tell me all about it, tell mummy, just tell mummy and I promise it won't seem as big any more I can help I can help I'm your mum I can help let me help please let me in come here my baby please don't cry.'

'I just can't let it go,' I heave.

'What darling? I didn't hear.'

'It's taken me over. It's all wrong. I can't get it out.'

'Shhh, darling, please, I can't understand what you're saying. Try and stop crying a bit, try and calm down so I can understand. Please, darling, please don't cry.'

Please don't cry. Lullaby. Please don't cry baby Lullaby.

Tell mummy just tell mummy.

Ha!

Ha hahahahaha.

Lullaby Lucy lullaby. Mum thinks she can help with a lullaby. Don't make me laugh don't make me fucking laugh or I'll be forced to...

'I can help,' she says again.

Pulls me to her. I don't stop her. I don't encourage her but I don't stop her. She can help, she continues to insist. She can help.

Just let her help.

But I just can't. I still can't do it. I just don't know how I will ever be able to. To do what I must. What everybody says I must do before I waste away and waste my life my self all the *promise* that I have shown. What can I tell her?

I could tell the truth, I suppose.

That I'm a fool.

That you have made a fool of me. Less than eight weeks of our being together and yet, three months after it all ended, I am holding in my piss during the night because I hate returning after a loo trip to an empty, quiet bed, without your wriggling and your snoring.

Oh, fuck-a-duck, the way you snored. I went a little crazy with frustration, squirming in protest until you were woken too, indirectly, by your own noise. And then the inevitable would happen, the usual touchy, giggly antics. And frustration gave way to desire, and desire gave way to satisfaction, and after that? Well, after that, the snoring diminished for a while, and I would sleep, contentedly (after *that*).

I try to recall the worst bits, and the end, to stuff myself up with anger and hatred, but guess what? They are nowhere to be found. All I can conjure is laughter, sex, discovery. And, of course, the shelter of you.

But you know what? I suspect I may be slap-bang in the middle of ruining my life. Because I don't know how I'm going to do it: I don't know how to let you go.

Which one of us was it though? Who *really* walked away? I have lost sight of what went wrong. If I knew exactly when or how, or which syllable it was that caused the shift, perhaps I could begin to understand, and from understanding to move to regret, and from regret to catharsis and from there make a new start, despite still wearing the scars of your inhabitation of me.

But I don't tell her any of this. Although I cry. I really cry. I let her hold me; we stand in the street just hugging and crying, crying and hugging and nothing more until she half escorts, half drags me back with her. Back home. This is home. Where I grew up. Where they still live. This is my home. I only realise it when I am sitting down at the kitchen table watching her peruse the contents of the fridge. I have a home again and I am eating scrambled eggs. Just a dollop of double cream in the egg mixture while you're stirring, mum always says. That's how to make perfect scrambled eggs. So that they melt inside your mouth.

'Dad is away so we can have a lovely relaxing evening,' she says. 'And there's no need to eat together around the table.'

I put on some old pyjamas that she has kept for nights like these, hoping that her last-born will come to stay. That I will need her again, like I did when a girl in the year above at school nicked my packed lunch and broke my specs. We eat the eggs on toast, on our knees in the sitting room. Mum lets me have seconds straight out of the saucepan. I think I'll test her patience — use my finger to catch the last flecks of egg that line the rim — but she makes no complaint.

'Dad is away,' she tells me again. 'So we can be as girly as we like.'

My mother smiles occasionally in my direction. A sad, perplexing smile. There is a lot of sadness between us tonight. At least the food tastes delicious and I realise how hungry I have been the last few weeks. How starving. I could eat another five scrambled eggs quite happily, but she has already done so much tonight that I don't want to ask for more. She does not push me any further; I think she is just pleased to have me in her possession; she is relieved that I have eaten and I am safe in pyjamas that are a bit tight around the chest. Mum double-locks the front door (because dad is away tonight, remember? So we had better take *extra precautions*). I hear her do it and say nothing. I am going nowhere tonight. Next we have all eyes on the television as we watch an old home movie of Christmas 1987 when my grandmother was still alive, screwing her eyes up to see if the turkey was cooked as well as hers, while my older cousin bossed everybody about, with them pretending to mind. Dad was thinner back then (and away far less often), while mum was chunkier, less angular. And me? I was only six, a flipping nightmare is what my mother calls that younger me, and I imagine her views have changed little over the years. The three of us so close, my parents like shoulderpads, smartening me up, puffing me out. But I can see it when I look now at my mother, the adulation for something, some*body*, that came from her own belly. At the side of her mouth and the side of her eyes and ears, that's where all the affection shows. It's all in the sides, at the edges of things, that is where we humans can see each other best.

On either side, at the periphery.

Acceptance. And the refusal to accept. Like that couple we saw in the café, you and I. That same reluctant need. That same belligerent devotion.

~~~~~~~~~~~~~~~~

But it happens (you return to me) as soon as I am left alone again. Mum goes to bed and I curl up in my old room, the one they now call *spare*.

I reach down beside the bed and from my bag I pull out a package that you sent me shortly before you left for Mexico, with the words 'eyes only' written in marker pen across the top left side. The package remains unopened but, finally, I rip the contents free.

But inside there are only pictures, so many pictures, snapped by a Polaroid. Smiles and eyes and legs and hands, nothing but body parts. Never the same part twice, but they are all a part of us.

And I know that you will think this a kindness, a signifier of our importance in your life, worth retaining in hard copy, and yet I find it neither kind nor gracious. With these pictures, you are returning us to me. I doubt you kept a copy for yourself. You pulled my heart out from up your sleeve. Made a show of all your magic and then you threw me in the bin.

I love you.

I love you.

I thank you for showing me love.

I hate you for showing me love.

You've shown me that loving you makes hating you easy.

But love

and hate are

Useless to me now, just as you are.

- Love,
- hate,
- compassion,
- ~~rejection, fear,~~
- honesty,
- truthtruthtruthtruth?

These words, these concepts, they act like thick paper dividers, in the foolscap files of our minds.

Goodbye.

Good   bye.

I love you. I loved you or I don't know; I thought I did.

I you = we = nothing no thing no.

The thing is that I still see your naked body in my dreams. But you are lying with someone else. Someone sweeter. Someone who will fight for you and not fear too much their half-chewed heart.

And yet I'm thinking to myself: it could have been worse. Could have been pregnant just like mum feared. Your baby, our baby: the product of our fanatic copulation. The end result of my employment under you. Could have got rid of it, the baby, in the same way you got rid of me and I can't rid myself of you.

I could instead, I suppose, be pregnant with it now. In readiness to give it up for adoption. Or I could have been intending to keep it. Like I didn't keep you. *Because* I didn't keep you.

How many Mexican women will you fuck, I wonder.

Once you've finished fucking Nancy that is. I presume that's what's going on. Or maybe you're just *travelling companions*. Just *friends*. Or just friends who fuck. Whatever it is, it is not *just*.

It is so clean and comfortable in this spare room, and very dark as well. Miraculously, I sleep very deeply. In fact, I sleep and sleep until mum wakes me at about eleven with some coffee, asking me what I'd like to eat.

'I'm not hungry,' I say.

I have slept too long, forgotten too long, and now my gut is filled with remembering; it overflows and makes me sick.

'Well,' she sighs. 'I'll be just downstairs. There's plenty of food. Just in case you have a change of heart, okay?'

'Okay.'

A change of heart.

Yes, that's what happened. *Is happening* perhaps.

'Maybe you should get away for a few days, even a week,' she says nonchalantly. 'Think about how you want to move forward from here. With work, your friends. With life.'

She tries to sound as if she is simply tossing an idea casually in my direction.

But I know my mother better than that.

'Yeah, maybe.' I yawn, and turn over as if to return to sleep.

'All right.' She walks away.

But my eyes are still wide open. 'Mum?'

She turns back. 'What?'

'I love you.'

'I know you do, darling.'

'I really love you.'

'I know, my darling, okay? So come downstairs and have some food, why don't you? Then maybe after that you'll feel like talking. Get up now, sweetheart, it's late.'

And so I do. Just like that. I go downstairs just as I'm told and eat some toast, spread with Marmite, refusing the offer of muesli, too heavy for a stomach stuffed with sleep. And, although I still taste little, with every bite the sickness diminishes. I feel the tingling of my toes, and it feels mischievous to be eating again, so soon after my last meal. It is like coming out into the light, this naughtiness, and I am tempted to try a smile.

~~~~~~~~~~~~~~~

Weeks pass in a vacuum. Summer gets hotter. Hotter and hotter. A heatwave, the highest recorded temperature in the centre of London since records began. Some twat clocks it as 52 degrees Celsius on the number 8 bus and 47 on the tube. You can't transport cattle in more than 28, so now people are angry, making a fuss. Some are even dying, the newsreader says, from heat exhaustion. But I am coming alive again. Only in the tiniest of ways. Something about this heatwave has nudged me into a state of almost living. The sun is so strong in the morning that it burns through my eyelids and opens me up unwillingly into the day. I start wearing an eyemask to sleep in, but still it burns and burns and I sweat and sweat until I have to wake up and at least acknowledge that there is light.

Next thing I'm ironing my shirt before I put it on. I even straighten my hair one morning, without thinking, before heading out and off to work. I think I smiled at a customer. I think he may have smiled back.

I check my emails. Even reply to a few. I read a novel. Something about it captures my contracting gut. Think maybe it is the emptiness and the guilt. The author must have felt it too; there is no way she could have written like that unless she felt that helplessness herself. The story is about this woman who loves this guy and then he dies and she can't grieve properly for him because all she is is this bloke's mistress. Which devours her inside. And she was already pretty fucked up before all this stuff happened, a sufferer of the eating *business*, anorexia nervosa, dysmorphia and all else that comes as a side order (green salad, and hold off on the French dressing). Anyway, the narrator gets pretty close to the edge but in the end she chooses life. However small the chink of light, she can still see it. A few months ago I would have called such symbolism crass. I would have spat on stories about anorexic slags who could not cry, and pointed out that malaria kills hundreds of people — hundreds of mistresses and hundreds of unfaithful husbands — every day. But now such things appear incomparable, and this book? It gives me hope and it gives me strength, which estranges me just one bit more from my despair. It is by a Scottish lady called Janice Galloway, entitled *The Trick is to Keep Breathing,* and I think yeah, hell yeah, that's what the trick is.

A week later I return to the bookshop where I bought it and pick out another paperback, which is stacked nearby. I take a quick look at the back but I already know I'm going to buy it because all the multi-coloured dots on the white front cover are so childishly defiant that I'm sure I will like it.

Perversely uplifting. Almost mythic, says *The Observer.*

I read the title again as I meander up towards the till.

A Million Little Pieces.

It is by James Frey; he's described as an ex drug and alcohol addict, which it turns out is not *all* true even though the book is heavily marketed as non-fiction.

A Million Little Pieces.

I read it. I love it. I cry when the book ends and go straight back to the beginning. I read it four times straight through. The only reason I don't read it a fifth time is because I never want it to get boring. James (the real James or the false one or the half real one — who cares?) had been broken so many times that everybody said he would never mend. But all these pieces, all these millions of pieces, meld back together, by luck, by love, by a power greater than James himself, and these same pieces form to make a different shape. It all makes sense. It gives me hope. And I feel lucky to be alive again. Just for a millisecond. But it is enough. It is enough.

~~~~~~~~~~~~~~~~

It is late August and I am on a train, stirring a cup of Nescafé. Middle-aged brown almost trips over the edge of the cup as the train rushes past dull flatness made more inspiring by ugly houses. Probably woke the residents up, I think, and try to force away the image of a feeble old man lying in bed, listening to the rattle of his false teeth in their container while the 08.21 sprinter blasts past.

Hey! Train! Don'tspillthecoffeeforChrist'ssake!

That was close.

I sigh.

I know I shouldn't empty another mini-carton of milk in there — don't do it — know it will spill all over that woman's satin and cheapen it with the baseness of its brown. But it's just so damn tasteless and I really need to caffeinate, just the act of ingestion, to convince myself that in some small way I am being woken by a substance, or a view, or a word, snatched only for me. Because I am aching for sleep, still drafting nightmares in the tunnels of my mind. Nightmares about when and how and why oh why yes why we felt the disobedient anaesthetic of a change of heart.

I keep stirring the coffee, as if I can dissolve the past, and with it dissolve you.

But already I know it: that the coffee will be just another stimulant, which exhausts me on its way through, leaving the past behind to rot among the dregs of me. I take a sip, holding some liquid beneath my tongue, next to that sinewy part, the part that people can only see if you decide to show them. Then I swallow, just before the burn, because I'm a wimp; I prefer to swallow quickly than have to spit the whole lot out.

We used to have a private joke about that, you and me. But now I'm just choking on coffee instead. On a train to god knows where, looking for god knows what.

I suppose a part of me is still looking for you. Which makes me worse than stupid because I'm not even crossing any kind of sea, let alone the Atlantic, and you are still in Mexico right now.

Still. I've always had a terrible sense of direction.

The man opposite has eczema inside his nose, just like you did. Little bits of flaky skin at the bottom of his nostrils.

I want to ask him if they annoy him, those little flakes. You always said it was so itchy, eczema.

The train hurtles on, exhausting me with its jolt-this-way-then-the-next, clattering past fields and trees, mocking them with its speed. One of the fields has maize growing in it, and every stalk looks for a second like it is moving backwards because the train moves on so fast. In another of the fields, rape seed is growing and then for a long while after all the crops in all the fields have been ploughed. And I wonder whether it would be crass to read anything into that. To regard it as symbolic of this sudden uprooting? Of *you*, yanking me right out from where I was and tossing me aside where I can no longer grow.

No, it wouldn't really be too crass. Not if it were correct. But this was hardly a marriage, and nobody has died. You are alive, almost unexpectedly, and I too am alive. (At least I think I am.)

I think therefore I am?

I drink therefore I am?

I shop therefore I am?

Whatever takes one's fancy, therefore one is.

Me? I get on a train I hope will take me miles away from all this *stuff* and drink instant coffee (whose primary ingredient is chicory, don't-you-know?) and think about buying a sandwich I know will taste of cardboard (even though I've never tasted cardboard), just to pass the time with chewing because I can't read can't hear the music I used to love shooting through my eardrums with headphones that wrap around my lobes...

... therefore I am?

So. This is hardly a disaster, is it? There are many routes that lead to separation, I think to myself, inspired by a fork in the track. This train takes the left, and outside the landscape changes, covered now with forests full of conifers.

I chew beyond the cuticle of my thumb, and tear off threads of skin, exposing more nail.

Where are you now, I wonder again. Right this very moment. What are you looking at? And whom? Still Nancy, or, if not, what is her name? Which part of her exactly are you looking at? And what's the name the two of you are giving to that part?

I am scribbling onto a newspaper, although there is no space for any more words, thoughts or ideas than those already printed. But if I turn the page onto its side? There's room for a small word in there; there's space for 'and' or 'two' or 'you'. I hug the pen tighter so as to control retching letters, which choke from its nib. They curl around a hole in the margin, a buffer around my heart.

And then I wipe my hand across my mouth, where saliva has gathered a little, and smell my skin, and then I think that's funny, that's odd, because there's a scent there, yes, there's a tang, and I don't think it comes from me.

It is pathetic. I have washed so many times since, and still I smell you on my skin. And so I make the same movement again, hand across mouth, but now I've wiped you away.

Remember the way we once joked haughtily together about ending it all, each of us desperate for the final, cocksure laugh, for the applause to fold over us? I smile, in spite of myself, as I remember the way we performed for one another. I am wondering when it was that you next washed the sheets. How soon after our last time in your bed did you soil those sheets with the blankness of hygiene?

Next time, I think; next stop is mine and next time I promise that I will be more careful of my heart.

At last the train pulls into Abergavenny. Walking up the platform towards the taxi rank, I look around. There is nothing here of any note. The surrounding countryside is neither majestic nor quaint. It is nothing more than dull, and I am disappointed, but not for long because suddenly my nostrils get a fright as they admit the dampness of the air.

There it is; if I can smell it in the air then it must all be hidden here somewhere. The wet. The rough, green ridges smothered with lovely, squelchy mud on those pitiless hills I hope to hike.

The Hikers' B'n'B: *nestled conveniently close to the various public footpaths that lead up and around in all directions.*

I have no idea what to expect really, except a bed and hopefully a basin. There are plenty of these places in this area, all stuffed with outdoorsy types who vacate during the day and return dirty, proud and noisy to the shower before refuelling in the pub. It was the name that attracted me to this particular place. Simple. Unimaginative. Anonymous and yet prescriptive: non-hikers shall not be welcome here.

It feels like we have been driving for half an hour but the clock says it is only ten minutes. The taxi stops at the beginning of a track.

'Can't drive down there, I'm afraid,' the driver explains. 'The Hikers' is the furthest on the left. That'll be eight pounds and ten, thanks.'

He holds his hand out for the cash. I hand him a note. Tell him to keep the change. I pick up my rucksack from the ground before starting to trudge down the track. After a hundred yards or so the smell of vegetable oil and deep fat frying assaults my nose. Nearly there. I can see the buildings now, all the same style although slightly different shapes. Same grey, same pebbledash, same white signs nailed above the door with only words to differentiate them. I look right to left: *Evergreen Guesthouse, The Settle Inn* and *The Hikers' Bed and Breakfast.*

And I admit it to myself: you had the right idea. Next time maybe

I'll take a leaf out of your book and go somewhere like Mexico to lose myself. So much more colourful than Wales. Not a speck of pebbledash in sight. But I am here now, so what the hell? I think I'll take a little stroll.

Where are you walking now? I wonder. We did not walk much, you and I. Just stayed in the bed, on the sofa, against the walls, fooling around with each other's hearts.

~~~~~~~~~~~~~~~~

On my third day in Wales I feel that I am ready to climb a mountain. It's not a huge one but it will do and, armed with a heavy rucksack full of provisions and pieces of extra clothing, I start to trudge along the footpath that leads away from the guesthouse.

All around the earth is plastered over with dew, and within half an hour my trainers are soaked through. Undeterred, I continue, wondering how much time must reasonably elapse before I can nibble on my first chocolate bar. I pass a few people along the way who appear to have already climbed the great hill and be on the journey back. It is only midday – hardly an unreasonable time to begin a walk – yet a couple of them administer frowns in my direction as they pass.

Soon I am beginning my ascent. The raindrops are made violent by the wind, and scrape against my cheeks, but I continue up up up, step after step after step. The water soaks me until I am mildew, smelling of mould and longing for relief. But the gusts only increase the higher I go, and there is no one coming down the mountain now, just me me me putting one foot in front of the other thinking of you you you and

the more it hurts the better it feels

the more it hurts the worse you are

the more it hurts the wetter I am the more I battle against the wind and rain (more like sleet, the higher I go) and cold, colder, I think, than I've ever been – the more I feel you seeping out of my pores.

But there is a new smell now, coming from the left, a stench of burning leather or something similar. It reveals itself like a crack in the wall; now that I have noticed it I cannot help but be aware of it, and it gets bigger with every step. So I detour from the path and follow my nose (which has forever been my problem). First leather, then burnt lasagne, racing up my nostrils and tickling the drops of water that have settled there. And after that smoke — not wood smoke (that genteel, Christmassy kind) but rather a harsh, apocalyptic kind of smoke.

I remember this feeling. This sense of unease. Guilt. Complicity. It is the same feeling that I get when the guy is tossed onto the bonfire with whoops and cheers to help him burn. But it is late August, over two months until 5th November, and there are no delighted squeals in this deadened place.

And yet the stench! It lures me onward. My curiosity takes me to all sorts of places and now it has brought me here, to this simmering heap whose core seems to be huge brown lumps, chunks of tree perhaps.

The rain is virtually victorious over the fire. Whatever it is has only been half destroyed: a mix of ashes and...

Wait!

As I get closer, pinching my nose, I see that these are bodies, of a sort.

A mix of ashes and flesh then.

They are cows. And bulls maybe. It is harder to tell the difference when they are dead and being roasted. I could probably make a guess nearer the end, supposing the bulls take longer to go, there being far more bulk to burn.

But there's the stench again; it grips tightly around my nose, forcing me back. Mustn't go too close; it isn't safe, all this ash-dappled flesh. First I notice legs that shoot out of the fire like flares. The hooves on the end of them, would they take more or less time to burn than the rest of the body? I wonder.

And I remember that café. That couple. With me not saying much except:

The generic term for hooved. 8 letters.
Try ungulate?
And then:
I never knew that about you — that you used to want to be a vet.
Well, that's because I never told you.

And, thinking about it, there are plenty of things that you still don't know about me. You'd never guess what I'm thinking now for instance, that I'm wondering what you would smell like — what part of you would take longest to burn — if you were thrown upon that fire.

For the cows, yes, it might well be their hooves. For me? I expect my gut would take the longest. Stuffed and knotted as it is. The last thing left of me before I was nothing more than cinders.

It is past mid afternoon; I should be heading back. But instead I slump myself on a wet rock nearby and watch the cows burn for over an hour, waiting for somebody to come, looking out for further clues. Nobody is manning the declining fire; it is wet enough that there must be virtually no risk of danger. A stiff mist is settling slowly but I am fairly sure that the whole area is deserted. The animals have been left, simply to burn. All I can guess is that this has something to do with the latest outbreak of Foot and Mouth that has swept across England and Wales. And as it falls onto various different surfaces — rock, grass, grit and my clothes — the rain sounds like a gamelan orchestra. An Indonesian treat on a Welsh mountaintop.

What an energetic, disorderly world this is.

The dusk is folding over me.

Your mouth.

Your hands. The way you touched my neck first, whenever we awoke.

Your hair, always spiked up like miniature alpine peaks.

Your *way*. The way you wrapped me up like a mummy then, when you had had enough, quickly unravelled me so that I rolled and rolled and rolled.

I stand and look out. The last of the daylight aims at me and shoots through the storm like a laser.

Again I see the cattle heap below, the smoke curling up towards me.

Your smile. How it changed your face, reduced your age.

The fire is reducing; their hides have disintegrated and it is just the last, tough pieces of meat that will still burn.

Your jokes, so funny at the time.

I stay still for a while, and watch. Wait, for nothing. Wonder if this is what it feels like to be In The Clear: no longer feeling a constant need to turn around (someone is watching me, following me) only to discover, each time I do, that there is nothing there.

~~~~~~~~~~~~~~~

It is time to begin the descent back to the guesthouse. The path is slippery and I fall over three times, skidding a few metres down. The second time a bottle of water flies out of the pouch on the side of the rucksack and rolls off somewhere it can't be chased. The third time my elbow grazes against a pointed fiend, a little blood betraying that I am hurt. It is a sharp blade; I am very lucky not to have been badly cut. I pick the whole thing up. It is about fifteen inches long. I smooth my thumb very lightly against its curved edge. I have seen one of these before, on a school geography trip to a working dairy farm. It is the kind of saw used for slicing the horns off cattle.

I put the saw inside my rucksack; I don't know why, I just need to keep it.

I don't know where I'll put it when I get home. It will look very out of place on my mantelpiece, next to the framed photo of my parents' wedding day.

There is nothing else to be done but to continue walking down the hill. I am feeling more confident now that I have this new weapon in my bag, and increase my stride by about a quarter. I am relieved when I reach the track that leads back to the guesthouse. My clothes are so wet they are chafing at all points where two limbs join. It should not take more than another half hour's walking to get back to warmth, and I am projecting to the moment I ease my body into a bath full of hot water, so hot that it will scald before it soothes.

I lean back against a boulder and scrabble about for a torch. Congratulate myself for remembering to bring one. But when I switch it on there is no light. I fiddle about with the battery for a few minutes but nothing works; I will have to continue along the path in the dark.

It's funny though, the dark. It brings me back to where things start. Not the beginning of the world or anything as grandiose as that. Just the beginning of me. My beginnings. That is always where I end up. All good stories are in some sense circular, I reflect. And my beginnings were with her. My mother, the woman who gives me all she has and who, after depleting her own store, would steal from others to give me more. She would have almost certainly brought spare batteries now, wouldn't she? And she would hand them over without a fight.

I have been running away from my own beginnings. Tearing myself out of the soil. Making myself dead. It goes against the natural order of things, exhumation. I thought that if I burrowed down low enough I could root you out, but it is not so. I cannot remove you from my past without removing her and all the others. I make a choice; I choose to exist, burdened with all that life incurs. You? You are miles and

miles

a

  w

    a

      y

and I can't remember why I loved you quite so much, or if I did or what we did or how we did... just titbits of joy and sadness and despair, and now it arrives within me like a tsunami: the result of a disaster that has occurred elsewhere, earlier, but produces results that will now swamp me without apology, this tidal wave of feeling, of everything I know or have known to be love so mixed and mingled so confused and inappropriate now welling up from my wet feet, it is you and it is me, it is you and it is them, those others who have mattered in alternative ways to how you mattered, to the *matter* that was Us. Urrrrrrrrgggggggggggh, it drags me it drags me it drags but I can't stop it, moving all the way up my legs my thighs, tickling my bottom, vagina, bowels before pushing the desire up up up into my gut into my stomach into my throat my neck and spilling out of my mouth, the words are spilling out, and you have gone you've gone where have you gone but now on my knees I am yelling, yelling yelling yelling that I want to go home.

I want to go home. Get me home.

'Want to go home, take me home!'

But nobody can hear me of course because they have all, quite sensibly, finished their day's walking before the light gave out. No more fire, no cattle. No great blast-off sending you out into the space outside my life. Just the slow absorption of responsibility and truth. Acceptance, pain and the imperfections of my past.

So. I must now pay for these wanderings. My reality-cheque, the transaction about to take place. I continue walking through the sludge. One foot in front of the other, one foot and then the other, one foot, the other. Other? No, there is no *other*; there is just one foot and then the *other*. Where am I now? Who am I with? I am in the Brecon Beacons while everybody I love and who loves me thinks that I am in northern Scotland because I lied. And why? Call it a no-reason lie. Every now and again we all need one, a temporary recklessness, a false and ugly power. In this same vein I have left my mobile phone in the guesthouse, determined to achieve total isolation, complete independence, not needing to need anything or anyone.

But now that I have it I hate it.

TOTAL ISOLATION?

COMPLETE INDEPENDENCE?

Grossly overrated, that's what they are, and I'm thinking back to that ashen cattle heap, hoping now that my gut would burn efficiently and without protest, and instead that my fingertips might fight the flames, my fingertips that touch, my fingertips, so sensitive, the very edges of me that can reach to any other and make contact. That is what I wish to keep hold of until the very last.

In reaching out we may get burnt.

But at least we feel. At least we touch. And that is better. That is enough, don't you think? Yes, more than enough. I hear you whisper your agreement to me from across the Atlantic, your voice, kind and apologetic, calling out to me, promising, *Lucy Fry, you're In The Clear.*

And I wonder whether you mind. I wonder if it is true.

Notes on Contributors

Heidi James

Heidi is a recipient of the Sophie Warne fellowship. Her publications include: the novel *Carbon* (2007), published by Wrecking Ball Press; a collaboration with photographer Tara Darby and designer Damien Poulien, *We are Only Human* (2007); and short stories in *Paris Bitter Hearts Pit, Dreams That Money Can Buy, Ambit, The Off Beat Generation, City Sickness, Open Wide Magazine* and *Full Moon Empty Sports Bag*. She is Arts Editor of *3:AM Magazine* and the proprietor of Social Disease Press.

Kay Sexton

As well as writing for the UK's premier sustainability journal, *Green Futures*, Pushcart-nominated Kay Sexton has recently completed 'Green Thought in an Urban Shade', a collaboration with the painter Fion Gunn that explores and celebrates the parks and urban spaces of four cities in words and images. 'Green Thought' was given residencies and exhibitions in London, Dublin and Beijing. Kay blogs about writing fiction at http://writingneuroses.blogspot.com/ and has a regular column at www.moondance.org.

Lucy Fry

Lucy remembers when she first decided she wanted to be a writer. She was eight years old, and set her sights on being published, at the very latest, by the age of ten. Since then she has fought with words, sometimes obsessively and sometimes waywardly. Much has been written — the good, the indulgent and the utterly unworthy — but from this novella she hopes that something superior will grow. Lucy has two degrees in English literature, a mild caffeine addiction, a job that makes her smile, and once jumped out of a plane at 12,000 feet with a large Australian strapped to her back. She is twenty-five (although, sadly, not for much longer).

Lightning Source UK Ltd.
Milton Keynes UK
23 November 2010

163302UK00001B/11/A